SHUTTER HOUSE

RICK WOOD

BLOOD SPLATTER PRESS

ABOUT THE AUTHOR

Rick Wood is a British writer born in Cheltenham.

His love for writing came at an early age, as did his battle with mental health. After defeating his demons, he grew up and became a stand-up comedian, then a drama and English teacher, before giving it all up to become a full-time author.

He now lives in Loughborough, where he divides his time between watching horror, reading horror, and writing horror.

I Do Not Belong

Death of the Honeymoon

Blood Splatter Books

Psycho B*tches

Home Invasion

Anthologies

Roses Are Red So Is Your Blood

Twelve Days of Christmas Horror

Twelve Days of Christmas Horror Volume 2

Sean Mallon:

Book One – The Art of Murder

Book Two – Redemption of the Hopeless

The Edward King Series:

Book One – I Have the Sight

Book Two – Descendant of Hell

Book Three – An Exorcist Possessed

Book Four – Blood of Hope

Book Five – The World Ends Tonight

Non-Fiction

How to Write an Awesome Novel

Thrillers published as Ed Grace:

The Jay Sullivan Thriller Series

Assassin Down

Kill Them Quickly

PART I

DON'T MIND ME

No matter how many times she attempted to blink, her right eye would just not open.

Her left eye was fine. A dollop of blood had dribbled into it, but a succession of blinks had fought the blood away.

The blood in her right eye, however, had been there for so long now it was beginning to crust.

He couldn't help but chuckle. She looked like a pirate on a budget. He wanted to make her say "yargh" and curl her finger into a hook, but he was barely able to get a word in amongst all the damn screaming.

Though the screaming wasn't the most irritating thing about her. That would be how, amongst her colossal cascade of shrieks, a flicker of her saliva had landed on the sleeve of his Armani suit.

"Do stop shouting," he instructed.

He did have an apron handy for when the fluids really started flying, but hadn't thought to wear it quite yet – who'd have thought a bludgeon to her head and a few screams would damage his suit?

"Shut up!" he grunted at the shouting girl who had the

audacity to not only spit upon the fine silk adorning his arm, but to ignore his instruction and continue to bang on with the same old *stop please stop,* and *just let me go,* and *oh no please no I'll do anything.*

Because, well – she won't do anything, will she? For example, she wouldn't willingly *die* to be let go – therefore, she would not do anything.

Stupid, stupid girl.

"I said shut up!" he repeated, with added conviction.

Her screams stopped but some annoying, quiet, incessant pleading persisted.

"Please, I promise I won't tell anyone, just let me go, please…"

I wonder if I could make it to Kensington for dinner, I do love their restaurants. I'd need to use the helicopter to get to London in time, mind…

"I won't tell anyone, I won't, please…"

My black slim fit silk Jacquard evening jacket would be perfect for that. I did prefer the blue one, but I do not like the idea of being seen in something that was on sale…

"I won't, I won't tell anyone…"

Although it would have gone so well with that checked shirt…

"Please, I won't say anything!"

"Yes, yes, I heard you the first time," he said, unable to believe that she was still bloody nagging. She was like an annoying little sister, constantly pulling on your sleeve, begging for you to do something with her.

At thirteen years old, he'd ripped his little sister's ear lobe off and made her tell Mother and Father she got it stuck in her friend's bike. Her friend got a jolly good rollicking from Father, but the little bitch never bothered him again.

"My parents… They have money…"

He snorted. An unpleasant laugh that even he himself felt a little repulsed by.

"I doubt it," he said mockingly.

"I won't tell—"

"Oh shut up, Sindy, you are getting rather tiresome."

Where was that damn apron?

Normally he'd take a little longer, try to savour it – but, honestly, this girl was starting to get on his nerves. He liked the screams – that's why he'd made sure that the shutters were sound proof – but nagging was the worst. He could take the odd *aaaaaah*, and *holy fuck that hurts...*

But just constantly going on and on and on and on?

No, thank you, M'am.

He found his apron resting against the leg of his Marylebone solid oak coffee table, on top of his forceps, vascular clamps and organ holders. He tutted at himself for the impudence.

"Of course," he muttered.

He placed his apron over his head. Beneath the lettering *Cambridge Alumni*, it was transparent; that way he could still see his pristine suit beneath the splatters.

"What are you going to do to me?" she asked.

He looked at her with purpose. He took her in, soaking up every little detail. Her blond hair had gone all bloody and scraggly from where he'd first hit her. Her eyes were still a little dozy, possibly from concussion, circling in and out, almost out of time with each other. Her rosy cheeks were flushed with red, her arms were shaking betwixt the rope, and by golly she hadn't even seemed to have realised she was naked yet!

"Please... I'll do anything..."

Again, he found amusement in her words.

She would do anything, though she probably wouldn't do it willingly.

He scanned her, starting at her throat, dragging his eyes down her bare torso, past the hairy mound and down her scarred legs. Honestly, he felt a little disappointed.

5

She must just have dressed well. She wasn't anywhere near as attractive as he expected her to be. Her breasts were petite pyramids, which he liked, but they were askew, poking in different directions. That may be just the way she was led, or maybe it was a childhood deformity, who knows? But her belly was so thin when she breathed inwards the outline of her ribs pressed against her skin like they were bursting to get out. There was no sensuous curve of the thigh; just two unshaped sticks in blemishes and scars from an adolescence of self-harm.

He sighed.

Wasn't what he'd hoped for.

He glanced at his watch.

He could always make dinner, then pick up another girl afterwards.

"Right, Sindy," he said, placing some plastic bags over his Salvatore Ferragamo shoes. "Time is escaping us, I'm afraid. I'm going to have to do this quicker than I had hoped."

"Do what? What? What are you going to do? *What are you going to do?*"

The screaming started up again.

He rubbed his sinus. He could feel a migraine coming.

Maybe I could pick up some Ibuprofen or migraine tablets when we land.

He lifted his axe, struggling under the surprise of its weight (usually he doesn't use something so big so quick) and held it above his head. She tried scampering away, like a mouse searching for its hole, piteously leaving a silly flailing leg behind her. He enjoyed the snap of her ankle as the axe fell through, sticking into the wooden tile beneath.

Her scream was so loud it almost broke her voice, like three hoarse voices pulled together into one gargantuan scream.

Then again, do I want to be taking migraine tablets if I'm going to be drinking...

It took some muscle to get the axe back out of the floor, but he managed. He wiped a few lines of blood off its blade and onto his apron, grinning at the sight of the few remaining tendons helplessly clutching onto her wayward foot.

Ah, screw it, I'll just get someone to go out and get some for me if I need it.

He lifted the axe up high, and this time brought it down upon her buttocks. Then he lifted it and smacked it into her back. He took particular pleasure in watching as her body spasmed, as her nervous system reacted to the fracture of her spinal cord.

He withdrew the axe one final time and took a few steps to her head. She was no longer struggling, and the screams had stopped; but there was still a croak, a wheezing outward breath, like something was deflating inside of a box that he just couldn't find.

He brought the axe down on her neck and the wheezing stopped.

He checked his watch. A Breitling Chronomat 44, just like Father had worn.

Perfect, he had enough time to get starters.

He removed his apron, triggered the remote to raise the shutters, and took the lift down to his Mercedes.

PART II

HOW DARE HE?

2

Amber was not a stripper, as she kept reminding everyone; she simply worked behind the bar in a strip club.

Didn't seem to make a damned bit of difference to the clients, mind.

They would still raise their eyebrows at her, proposition her, calling her things like *babe* and *sweet-cheeks* as their eyes lingered on her breasts.

There was nothing more dismal than the day shift in the strip club. Of course, the night shift wasn't much better; the crowds were bigger, which meant the quantity of gropes against her buttocks were more frequent. It seemed as if all of the wandering, lecherous eyes that stared at her saw no difference between the hard-working girls grinding the poles, and the poor barmaid simply trying to make it to closing time.

But the day shift – *oh, boy*. There were barely any clients – just a few men in suits at one table and an old man at another; which should make the shift more bearable, but just made the place more depressing. And at least the girls who worked at night would have a laugh with her, using humour to make everyone's shift just that bit more bearable; the girls who worked the day shift barely granted their faces the luxury of a smile. Their drab appearance and poor tan lines and bloodshot eyes didn't bother Amber – it was the lack of comaraderie that bugged her so much. They were the ones who would glare at her and resent her because they were doing the hard work and she wasn't.

Yes, they were partaking in a far more strenuous occupation than Amber – but that was shown in the difference in their pay cheques. Whilst they could afford to rent the best flats, stroll around town in the most stylish clothes, and eat in the swankiest of restaurants – Amber could not. Her trek home would involve a stop at Aldi for a 99p cheese pizza, then taking it home and trying not to burn it as she made her sick mother tea – her sick mother for whom she was also a full-time carer.

The sick mother for whom she had dropped out of university for.

Unfortunately, the wages of a carer couldn't cover the mortgage. And, honestly, her meagre wage at *Syphy's Strip Club* didn't do much to help either.

Even the name of the strip club perplexed her.

Syphy's Strip Club.

Yes, the owner was called Syphy, but most clients wouldn't know that – and all Amber could think, every time she scoffed at the sign on her way into work, was how close it was to *Syphilis Strip Club.*

Not that you'd point it out to Syphy, mind. Not that he wasn't approachable – he was incredibly approachable, in fact. He just didn't particularly look at your eyes and listen to what you had to say.

"Hey, doll," said some guy at the bar who looked like he still lived in his parent's attic, slamming his empty pint glass on the bar. "How's about another beer, yeah?"

Doll?

She took a big, deep breath, decided it wasn't the worse thing she'd been called, and let her deep breath go. She took his glass and poured his drink.

"That will be four seventy-five," she requested, adorning the same wretched smile she forced to her unwilling face every damn day.

"If we call it an even ten would you show us a tit?"

She tried not to glare, willing the smile to stay on her face.

"That will be four seventy-five," she repeated.

"Or if I give you twenty will you show us both of them?"

"That will be four seventy-five," she repeated once more.

He handed over a five-pound note. As she went to take it, he held onto the other end. She looked at him, and he responded with a cheeky wink that made her feel like she was covered in grease. She pulled the fiver from his hand and turned to the till, where she jabbed the buttons and took out twenty-five pence change.

She held the change out, and he made sure to grab her hand and caress his slimy fingers down hers as he took the money.

She looked to the bouncer at the door. She could request some support.

But then again, what was the point?

The bouncer looked like a shrivelled old man approaching retirement. His face looked like the tip of her finger when she'd been in the bath for ages. If he actually took her side, he still couldn't do much.

"Thank you kindly," he said and re-joined his cocky mates. Even though his words were innocent, the way he said them felt loaded. Like he had the upper hand in a conflict she wasn't aware of. Like he was satisfied that he had made her feel disgusting. He returned to his laughing mates and leered over Honey; a single mother in her early thirties grinding her crotch against the pole, her eyes dying as she came toward the end of a double shift.

Amber looked to her watch.

Twenty minutes to go.

All the things she could do in that twenty minutes…

She could watch an episode of *Friends*. She could make her mother tea. She could go outside and give money to the beggar who lived in the doorway of the boarded-up factory next door.

Yet, here she was, wasting her life.

Away from her mother, who was probably coughing up blood over her blanket, waiting for Amber to return and take care of her.

Instead, there she was, motionless and manic, working for minimum wage in a place that made her want to scream.

She looked at her watch again.

Nineteen minutes.

Jesus…

3

AN EARLY EVENING HAZE HUNG OVER THE SKY, PROJECTING AN image of Amber's mood.

She glanced at her watch and forgot to look at the time. She couldn't wait to wash that shift off.

Just as she began to contemplate the length of her walk home, a familiar Nissan Micra chugged down the road and stopped beside her with an unidentifiable rattling noise that she ignored.

She smiled at the sight of Luke winding down the window. She had two older brothers, but Luke was the one who had stuck around. Not that her other brother had done anything wrong by leaving for university. After all, if Luke had never been excluded from school then he would probably have gone to university as well, he had the intelligence for it – but, then again, the cannabis-dealing business had done him well.

She just wished Luke didn't look so ill all the time. His skin clung to his bones, bags stuck beneath his eyes, and he always seemed to have a groggy, distant look etched across his face.

Nevertheless, he was her brother – and no amount of police

or concerned boyfriends could ever make her steer clear of him.

"Hey," he said, his voice weak and croaky.

"Hey, you."

"Thought you might want a ride."

"You are a saint!"

She bounced to the passenger seat. She had never been so grateful for a lift. He mustered a smile a little too wide and a little too long, then drove off.

"You should get another job," he said. "I know a few friends that went to that place. Said it was gross."

"Some friends, huh?" she teased.

He raised his eyebrows in response.

"I'd love to quit," she told him. "It's all I think about when I'm counting down the minutes, picturing the look on Syphy's face as I tell him he's a perve and he can shove it."

"Then why don't you?"

Amber ran her hands through her hair and wished it was that simple.

"You know why," she told him.

"Because of mum?"

A solemn mood abruptly descended; the same mood that always entered a room at the same time as reality.

"She'd do the same for us," she said.

"Would she?"

"Yes. Whatever you want to say about your upbringing, she gave us everything she could."

"Yeah..." he grumbled.

There was another unspoken subject: their dad. He lived in America now – or, at least, that was the last she heard. They all, as a unit, decided to cut ties with him almost five years ago. However much you want your father in your life, sometimes you need to remove toxic influences for the sake of your own sanity.

"Do you have any idea when Gray's coming back?"

"Oh, what, Mr Perfect?"

Ah, of course. Luke's resentment toward Graham. Any time Gray was mentioned, this was the reaction Luke had. She understood it, but at the same time, she didn't; they had both made their choices, Gray had just made better ones.

"Yeah, isn't his semester over now?"

"You know he's just going to leave again after the summer, right?"

"How do you know that?"

"He's applying to do teacher training. Which means another year away. Which means another year for us to deal with mum."

"If she lasts that long."

She regretted saying it as soon as the words passed her lips. For Luke's credit, he didn't let his face show how he felt.

But he didn't speak either.

They just continued the journey in comfortable silence, both of them lost in thought about the many ways things could be better.

As they stopped at a set of traffic lights, Amber was grateful to Luke for starting a new conversation.

"Look at this dickhead," he said, nodding at a car a few lanes over.

Amber saw the shiniest, slickest, smoothest ride she'd seen in a long time. A car that stuck out from every other car around it. She knew little about cars, but she didn't need to – she only needed to look to see that this car was impressive.

"Some wanker has enough money to buy a Mercedes," Luke ranted. "And we can't even afford medical costs. And it's a hatchback, too. How much do you think that cost?"

"I have no idea."

"Neither do I, but I tell you what, I bet it was shit loads."

"Probably."

"That car probably cost more than what we earn, all together, in a decade. No, probably a life time."

"Yeah."

She continued to stare at the car. Something about it gave her chills. The windows were blacked out, but then again, aren't they often blacked out on cars like that?

She wondered who was driving it. What they looked like. How they sounded. Whether they took care of their sick mother too.

The lights turned green and the Mercedes' acceleration was so loud that all the heads at a nearby bus stop turned to look.

"Show off," Luke mumbled. Despite driving, he never took his eyes off the car.

"Some people, eh?" Amber confirmed.

"Yeah, some people."

As the Mercedes drove toward the bus stop, it sped up. It veered toward the outside of the lane and drove through a puddle, a dirty puddle that left everyone at the bus stop drenched. Including a mother and child, an old lady, and a guy minding his own business, listening to headphones that were probably now ruined.

"The fucker," Luke snarled. He veered across the lanes until he was behind the Mercedes and sped up to match its speed.

"Luke, what are you doing?"

"What am I doing? I'm following this prick."

"Luke, please, come on."

"I'm going to teach him a lesson."

"Luke, let's just go home."

"Or at least I'm going to see where he lives."

Amber knew her brother well enough to know that when his temper took over there was nothing she could say to change it.

Later on, she would come to wish that she had tried harder to argue with him.

She would wish that she had made him turn back.

4

HE LIFTED THE NORMANN COPENHGAEN COGNAC TO HIS MOUTH and placed his lips around the Barwell Cut Crystad, welcoming the harsh sting of the alcohol against the back of his throat, drinking it down like it was milk to a baby.

He flicked across the next page of *The Independent*, tutting as he often sees people doing. There was another gentleman sat across the bar of the Sunnyside Hotel – he wasn't staying there, it was just one of his favourite bars – and saw how the gentleman shook his head at his copy of *The Guardian*.

Strange, the news never seemed that bad to him. There was news of another killing spree by some wayward teenager in America, a tsunami somewhere in a country he couldn't care less about, and a stock crash in–

A stock crash?

He shook the paper and looked again at the article.

Then he glanced at the date.

This newspaper was two months old.

He curled his lip and vigorously shook his head. He could feel himself getting more and more worked up, could feel his leg shaking in that way it did, his foot wagging as it balanced on his knee, his free hand grabbing onto his Jean Pierre Gold-Plated Tourbillon Cufflinks and pulling.

The impudence!

"Excuse me!" he called to a nearby waitress. Tall, slim, probably in her twenties, bottle-blond, attractive but a little chubby on the thighs.

"Yes, sir?" she asked. Her voice was so timid. Like she was scared to be talking to someone despite it being her fucking job.

"This newspaper is out of date."

"Oh, is it?" she asked.

This riled him. That was not the reaction he was hoping for. Where were the apologies? The grovelling? The offer of something complimentary to make up for the sheer lack of attention to the intricacies of her job?

"Yes. Yes, it is," he repeated, his voice stern and clear.

"We have more if you wish–"

"I could not give a damn if you had more," he responded, his voice quiet but deadly, calm yet devastatingly clear. "I picked up this one, and it made me worried by what I read."

"Would you like me to get you a new one?"

"No, I would not–" he looked at her name tag "–Daisy. I would not."

"Okay. Well, if you do, let me know."

"Don't you dare go anywhere. Have you any idea what you have done?"

"Sir, as I said, I apologise."

She walked away.

The foolish bitch walked away.

How dare she?

How fucking dare she?

He finished the last sips of his brandy, placed the newspaper neatly upon the table, stood, straightened his collar, and walked purposefully past the bar and into the street.

He looked up. A CCTV camera watched him step out of the hotel. He took a few steps until he was out of sight, then doubled back through a nearby back alley, circling the adjacent building until he was at an exit.

In that back alley, he waited.

Unnoticed. Untouched. Uncaring about the patience required.

It took around forty minutes but, eventually, she came out.

She didn't notice him at first, too preoccupied with taking a bin bag to the dumpster. As she turned to go back in, she noticed him and jumped.

"I'm sorry, sir, but you're not supposed to be back here."

He strode toward her without saying a word, took hold of the back of her hair, and drove her head into the dumpster, flinching at the rancid smell.

She blinked a few times, as if trying to pull herself from a daze. He took a clump of hair, dragged her to the brick wall of the alley, and he drove her head into it again, and again, and again.

He let her drop to the floor, pulled out his Robin Silk Twill Handkerchief – annoyed that he was going to ruin it but assuring himself he had more at home – and wiped a few splodges of blood from his right shoe.

Taking hold of her hair, he dragged the groggy slut across the rough surface, ignoring the moans as her distant mind acknowledged the pain of being dragged through the scrapes and bumps of a dirty alleyway. He had to pass more dumpsters and they stunk and he became so full of hatred for her because of it that he had to stop himself from killing her before he had his apron on.

He was *not* going to mess up his suit for her.

His Mercedes-AMG Project One, dark silver, hatchback, sat a few yards away from the alley's opening.

He dropped her hair, walked up to the boot and opened it.

He shoved a few things aside – his Base A20 GA Headset Headphones, a bag of spanners and other tools, and a wrapped birthday present he meant to give to his sister but never did and now he'd forgotten what it was. Probably some shit book about two people falling in love in dire circumstances, or a box of fancy chocolates she wasn't worth.

He returned to the alley and hoisted her over his shoulder. With one hand he kept her balanced, and with the other he held her head to ensure no blood spoiled his collar.

He looked back and forth from the alley and waited for some teenager with earphones in to turn the corner, and a runner wearing a green top and shorts so tight they should be illegal to pass. Then, with quick pace and expert precision, he placed her in the boot and shut it.

He took to the driver's seat, turned the key and listened to the engine purr. He pressed his foot upon the accelerator and spun around the corner.

As he approached a bus stop, he made sure to veer into the adjacent puddle, enough to drench all the people waiting for their transport. He chuckled as he watched them in the rearview mirror. So angry about such a little thing some guy in a Mercedes had done.

Little pleasures, eh?

He put in his favourite CD, and turn it up as loud as the car would allow. It was Josh Grobin's Bridges album, the deluxe version, and he fast-forwarded to track four: *Musica del Corazon*, featuring Vicenten Amigo.

Damn, he loved that song.

5

AMBER HAD ALWAYS BEEN THE VOICE OF REASON TO LUKE'S madness. His company had always made her feel safe in scary situations, but without his company she was far less likely to end up in scary situations.

Despite the clutching of the seat and the wide-eyed stare at the rear-end of the Mercedes, Amber was still a little intrigued.

As a child, she'd dreamt about living a life where everything was easy. Her mum was a successful business woman for most of her childhood, then struggled after she was laid off, and began to grow sick during Amber's adolescence. All her mum's savings had gone toward trying to maintain the life they knew, but that did little to stop the struggle. Amber would tell her mum it was fine, that she didn't need the new iPhone or latest clothes for Christmas, that she'd settle for some book that, deep down, she wasn't interested in reading. Then she'd go up to her room, climb into bed, close her eyes and imagine: being someone hugely successful, or a celebrity, maybe a pioneer or entrepreneur, someone who was an influence to all the other women in the world struggling to have their voices heard.

She'd earn so much money she'd be able to give loads away to charity and have it mean nothing.

And, most of all, she'd use her wealth to help struggling teenagers trying to take care of a sick mum.

Luke slowed the car down. They had been driving for almost fifteen minutes, yet it seemed like they'd entered a whole new world. Every house on the street could fit five of her mum's houses in. They were so far apart, gated, with driveways longer than many roads.

The Mercedes came to a stop outside of the biggest gate. A hand reached out and tapped a few numbers into a keypad, the gate opened, and the car drove inside, disappearing into a driveway surrounded by trees. Despite the large cluster of trees, the top of his mansion was still visible in the distance.

The gate closed and they were left outside, unknowingly glaring at the path of the car.

"Imagine," Luke said, quietly, almost to himself.

"Yeah," Amber conferred.

"Just…how come dickheads like him get places like this, y'know?"

"I know."

She saw that look on his face. The one she'd seen when they were at school and a teacher tried to tell him off, or another student made a comment that struck a nerve.

"Come on," she urged him, worried about where this was going to go. "We've seen where he lives. We can go now."

"How good would it be," he said, disregarding her rationality, "to teach this guy a lesson?"

"Is it worth it?"

"Fuck yeah, it's worth it. To show this arse-wipe that he don't own the world, that he don't own us, that he don't go spraying people at a bus stop just waiting to go to their boring jobs."

"Luke," she said, and he recognised the tone. When they

were at school, and he was getting worked up, the only thing that could calm him down was her. Sometimes teachers even went to another classroom to find her, knowing she was the only voice he'd listen to.

"Yeah, all right," he said.

She caught sight of the time in the dashboard.

"Oh, damn!" she exclaimed. "Mum's hospital appointment is soon."

"Her hospital appointment?"

"Yes, I'm taking her to Worcester General."

"Ain't that, like, two bus rides away?"

"Three. But we'll take the train."

"I thought the doctors said there's nothing else they can do for her. That it's all through her body."

"Yes, but that was Gloucester General–"

"And how many hospitals is that now?"

She huffed. She didn't want to hear it.

"This would be the fourth."

"Amber, man, you just got to let it go."

"Let it go? That's Mum you're talking about."

"I love her, and I'd do anything I could to help her – if there was anything I could do. But what you're doing, it ain't healthy."

"I… I have to try."

He sighed. Turned back to the steering wheel.

"It's not good for you," he spoke. She could hear true concern in his voice. Despite their faults, she was lucky to have some family that cared for her.

"And following a guy back to his house just because he soaked a bunch of people is?"

"The guy's a dick."

"And so what? What were you planning to do if there wasn't a gate there? Get out and pummel him?"

"Maybe."

"You have no idea who he is. He could be some psycho or have a weapon on him or something."

His eyes turned back to the gates, peering up at the top of the mansion, at the impressive architecture that encircled the top of this guy's oversized abode.

Resolved to let it go, Luke put the car in gear and drove away.

Finally, Amber let her breath go, unaware that she'd been holding it.

By the time Luke dropped Amber off and left to do whatever it was he did in the evenings – something Amber liked to remain blissfully ignorant of – they were already running late for her mum's hospital appointment.

"Mum!" she called out as she stepped through the door. She could smell the stench of a long shift clinging to her clothes like musk and she was desperate to change out of them. "Mum, I'm home!"

She didn't expect a response, of course. Her mother wasn't able to muster the energy to shout a greeting nowadays. It was just nice to let her know that she was home.

She picked up the mail and sorted through it. It was all bills, all final warnings, the same old stuff. She dumped them on the shoe rack and walked through, switching on all the lights.

She found her mum in the living room, sat in her chair, her head lolling on her shoulder, her eyes peacefully closed.

She hated this image. Not because her mum shouldn't have rest; she needed a lot of it. It was because whenever she returned from work to this sight she was never sure whether it was her mum resting, or her mum dead.

Amber wanted to voice her thoughts.

Wanted to shout her objections.

But the words just stayed in the prison of her mind.

"If you'd like to take a seat," the receptionist said, following a few beats of silence Amber wished she had filled.

Curling her lip and clutching her mum's wheelchair, she parked her mum and sat down.

She didn't realise how tired her legs had been until her bum hit the plastic cushion. It wasn't just the physical weariness of being on her feet all day or of pushing around her mum – it was the tension, the constant grip of her muscles, the constant shake of her legs.

Across from her was a woman, probably eighteen, about her age. She was slumped down in her seat, face like a smacked child, staring at the screen of her phone. Next to her was her mother, probably about Amber's mum's age, looking over her daughter's shoulder, trying to engage her in conversation she was unwilling to partake in.

Amber hated that girl.

Hated her for ignoring her mother. Hated her for not paying attention. Hated her for the attitude wiped across her face.

Amber wondered if, had her mum never fallen ill, she'd be sat here with the same posture and the same unwillingness to give attention to a parent who loved her.

She couldn't decide: was she hateful, or jealous?

"Elsie Michaels," said the voice of a doctor, a good-looking man in his thirties.

Amber took hold of her mum's wheelchair and followed the doctor, hoping that this time would be different to the rest.

After all, you know what they say...

Fourth time's a charm.

7

THE DOCTOR'S CREDENTIALS WERE PROUDLY DISPLAYED UPON HIS office wall: a first-class honours degree in medicine, a master's degree, his doctorate, and numerous other certificates displaying qualifications Amber didn't recognise.

Sparsely placed among these framed certificates were pictures; each featuring a smiling woman with long brown hair and a boy, a little older than a toddler.

Another picture of the child when he was younger sat proudly on the doctor's desk.

Amber closed her eyes and leant her forehead on her palm. She was getting a headache. She wasn't sure how much more she could take of other people's happiness.

The doctor entered and smiled at her, that reassuring smile doctors always have that never gives anything away. He sat in his chair across his desk from her, leaning forward and interlocking his fingers.

"Amber," he said. "How are you holding up?"

"What do you mean?"

"Well, I have worked with many young carers, and I have seen how wearing it can be. Are you taking care of yourself?"

Amber frowned. What did this have to do with her mum?

"I'm fine," she lied.

"If you would like some support–"

"I just want to know about my mum."

He sighed.

"I know, Amber, and I will talk to you about your mother in a moment. If I'm being honest, you look tired."

Amber considered her response, considered exploring her difficulties, her strenuous life and the pressure she constantly felt pushing down upon her, pushing on her shoulders, as if it was going to push her into the ground, further and further, until the roots took hold of her, pulled her under, and she could breathe no more.

As it was, she decided not to.

"I just want to know about my mum," she repeated.

"Okay," the doctor acknowledged with a false smile. He turned to his computer and clicked his mouse a few times.

She wondered what he was looking at and wished he would just give her the bad news already.

"I can see by her records that you've visited a few other hospitals."

"Yes."

"And what did they say?"

She huffed. What did this have to do with anything?

"They said that they couldn't do anything."

"I see," he said, continuing to scroll. "And you came here for…"

He raised his eyebrows, awaiting an answer.

How was she supposed to complete that sentence?

False hope?

Desperation?

A miracle?

"Another opinion," she finally decided.

"Okay," the doctor said.

She was starting to hate the way he said *okay*. It felt demeaning, as if he was belittling the way she felt, like he was saying *okay* rather than telling her she was an idiot.

"Unfortunately," the doctor finally said, "we don't have better news for you."

Every piece of false hope and spark of optimism drained out of her like the last gurgle of water down a drain.

"The cancer has spread through her. It's in her throat, in her lungs, in her arms, possibly even her intestines. I understand she's had two rounds of chemotherapy already?"

Slowly, she nodded, faintly and non-committal.

"It's pretty aggressive, and I don't think another round will work. In fact, I'm certain of it."

His words melded into the words of every other doctor.

So matter-of-fact.

So eagerly honest.

So patronising.

Different voice, same verdict.

She looked again at the photo of the child on his desk and decided that she truly, truly hated him.

"I would probably say that she had, maybe, three to five months. I think the best thing you can do is make her comfortable."

Make her comfortable?

Had he seen her mum?

Had he seen what she was like?

She was constantly moaning, waking up in agony, falling asleep because she couldn't keep her head up.

How the hell was she meant to be comfortable?

"I'm sorry I couldn't give you any better news."

No you're not.

You're not sorry.

You're going to go home, have tea with your wife and forget all about us.

"Thanks," she grunted. She lifted herself from the chair and trudged toward the door.

"You really should get some support for yourself," the doctor said.

She shut the door behind her.

She leant her head against the wall and pleaded with herself not to cry.

Not here.

Please, not here.

8

He sat back in his armchair, newspaper in hand, and gazed upon his masterpiece.

He was very good at what he did.

No, more than good.

He was the Picasso of what he did.

In fact, she looked like a Picasso painting, her eye too far from the other and her body distorted into a well-worked image of surrealism.

He took in a deep breath and let it go.

What a life this was.

He had it all.

The money. The house. The car.

The women.

The job.

He was the person other people craved to be. The person that interns would look to and think *damn, I wish I could be as successful as him some day.*

But most of all, it was his deep, deep passion for human mutilation and disfigurement that provided him with this wondrous happiness he experienced.

He stretched his legs out and placed them on her stiff rear end, stuck in the air from glorious rigor mortis, and opened the paper.

Even more satisfaction filled his thought at the sight of the main article on page 3.

POLICE PLEAD FOR WITNESSES IN MISSING GIRL CASE

SHEILA HAMSMITH, a twenty-one-year-old waitress at the Sunnyside Hotel, disappeared from her place of work at approximately 3.23 p.m. on Tuesday afternoon. The parents of Sheila, who lives with her fiancé, Devon, and her son, Charlie, are said to be increasingly worried for her safety

"IT IS JUST NOT LIKE HER," Caron Hamsmith, Sheila's mother, told us. "She's the most responsible person you would ever know. She would never go somewhere without letting someone know. She is a doting mother and would never abandon her son. The only thing we can think is that she has been taken against her will."

CARON WENT on to plead with any potential abductor. "Please, just talk to Sheila, and you'll see that she's a kind, loving woman, who would never hurt anyone."

HE SNORTED. Too late for that.

POLICE ARE APPEALING for witnesses who may have been at the Sunnyside Hotel during the afternoon of the incident.

. . .

THE WHOLE WORLD was running around like headless chickens, and he was sitting back and enjoying it.

"So," he said, "your name is Sheila, is it?"

He looked at her face, empty and stiff, broken by blood, her features skew-whiff, pointing in directions they should never point, mangled and tangled.

"Your mother sounds like a drag," he continued. "Gosh, I'm glad I didn't have to spend the evening with her."

He sighed.

This conversation was going nowhere.

It wasn't like she was going to reply.

He stood, growing agitated.

"Well there's no point me just stood here chatting to myself, huh!"

He dropped his face right next to hers and looked into the one eye he could.

"You selfish bitch. All I wanted was a little conversation!"

Still no response.

In a spurt of wrath, he lifted his axe and hacked at her once more. He chopped into her elbow, removing her forearm, then her knee, kicking her loose shin away.

He grabbed a knife with a rabid scream and stuck it into the underside of her breast.

It was so hard. He expected her arm and leg to be tough, but her breast was so hard. Like he was hitting clay or stone.

He stuck the knife in further and further, twisting and twisting.

He gave up.

The knife wasn't going in. His arms were tired.

But he wasn't done yet.

She was, but he wasn't.

He left the room to retrieve his mobile phone from beside his bed where it had been charging. He hit three and waited for speed dial to do its work.

"Hello, Best Bellas," came the eager reply of a woman too old for this shit.

"Hello, is Eve working tonight?"

"I believe so."

"Perfect. I'd like her to meet me at this hotel."

He was hot, he was half-full, and his night was only just beginning.

Amber felt a tinge of sadness, in the way that one does when witnessing a stranger's misery.

"She's the most responsible person you would ever know," stated Caron Hamsmith on the morning news. "She would never go somewhere without letting someone know. She is a doting mother and would never abandon her son. The only thing we can think is that she has been taken against her will."

They showed a picture of the girl. She looked younger than twenty-three. She could easily have been one of her friends. She was also a waitress, although worked in a far classier establishment than Amber.

"Is there anything you'd like to say to someone who may have taken her?"

Caron's eyes focussed on the camera, and Amber could feel them peering into her soul.

"Please, just talk to Sheila, and you'll see that she's a kind, loving woman, who would never hurt anyone."

She turned off the television and thoughts of the news report faded, replaced with thoughts of the day ahead.

She went to the clothes horse in the kitchen and felt her

blouse. It was still a little damp, but she'd worn damp clothes many times before. She put it on, did it up, and purposefully didn't look at her reflection in the window.

It was still better than what the other girls were made to wear.

She found her way to her mum's bed, in what used to be the conservatory but had since been changed to a bedroom. A heap of dried sick stained the pillow next to her.

A glance at the clock told Amber that she was already running late, but she had no choice – she couldn't leave dried sick there all day.

She helped her mum to her wheelchair, took her into the living room, and placed her in front of an episode of *Eastenders*; though the television could be showing any television program and her mum would have no idea. Amber collected the bedsheets and duvet and put them in the washing machine. She put the timer on for the afternoon, kissed her mum on the head, and left for work.

After another long bus ride she arrived at *Syphy's Strip Club*. She nodded the same hello to the same bouncer, forced the same smile at Syphy's same ill-timed remarks, and left her same bag in the same locker.

She leant against the till, staring out at the club, trying not to contemplate life but unable to do anything but. Two girls were flaunting what they had, one of them on stage, and one of them in the corner gyrating upon a man who didn't know how to keep his hands to himself. There were probably five customers in all. Besides the man having a hell of a time with Brandy, there were three young men sat around the stage and an old man sat at the bar nursing a pint of Stella. The old man was in here most days, and she had come to know him as Bill.

Unlike the others, Bill never had a lap dance and never made crude remarks. He was a regular like a pub would have a regular; probably lonely and left to grow old alone.

She wondered if she'd ever get to grow old.

She wondered if her mum…

She shut her eyes tight. This wasn't the place.

Still, she couldn't help but think: *four doctors.*

Four separate hospitals.

Four opinions that all happened to be the same.

There was only one hospital left within travelling distance, but it was private. It wasn't like she could afford it – she had a little left over from savings that she'd been working her way through to support her mum, and there wasn't much left.

Then again, it wasn't like she had much choice.

Knowing that no one would mind or even notice, she took out her phone and googled: *Cotswolds Private Hospital.*

The website alone was impressive. Pictures of smiling doctors and smiling patients, testimonies from those who'd had their lives saved, smiles from those who could afford such a thing.

It seemed so unfair.

Why should someone with money be more deserving of survival?

Bill grunted. That was his signal that he'd like another drink. She took his glass, placed it under the tap, and watched gormlessly as it filled.

She had little over a thousand left in her savings. She'd originally put it aside from a Saturday job working in a chip shop to pay for university. She'd once had enough to cover living costs until her final year.

But it didn't look like that was happening any time soon.

"There you go," she said, handing Bill his beer with a forced smile. His distant eyes avoided hers as he took the beer, gulping down at least a fifth of it in one.

She looked around to see if Syphy was watching.

The group in front of the stage all had relatively full drinks. They wouldn't be coming to the bar soon.

She had time. She found the number and called.

"Hi," she said to the receptionist who answered the phone – a woman who already seemed more accommodating than the receptionist from the other day. "I was wanting to know how much it would cost for a consultation... It's for my mum, she has cancer... Just for a check over..."

She waited to hear the cost.

"How much?" she asked, wanting to make sure she heard right.

Just a consultation: £1,100.

That was all she had left.

But what did her mum have left?

Three to five months, wasn't it?

It wasn't like she'd be needing to support her mum much longer. What good was the money going to be now?

"Do you have any appointments this evening?"

They had one at 8.30 p.m. with Doctor William Chesser.

Even the name sounded rich.

"I'll take it," she told them.

Her final try.

Then it occurred to her: but what if they could help her? How could she afford any further treatment they might provide?

Realising it was unlikely that they could, she decided she'd deal with the issue if she was lucky enough to have to deal with it.

For now, the appointment was enough.

Well, it wasn't enough.

But it was hope.

Even if she was the only one who had any left.

GRAY STOOD OFF THE TRAIN WITHOUT ANYONE TO MEET HIM.

What did he expect? It wasn't like he'd told anyone when he was coming home.

He wondered if anyone would show up even if he had.

He slung his bag over his shoulder and dragged his suitcase from the platform to the bus stop outside.

Three years of his life over, just like that. He hoped that he would get a first in his degree, and that, by this time next year, he would be a fully qualified History teacher.

Yet all that work felt like nothing as he returned to all the problems he had left.

He loved his mum dearly, but she wouldn't have wanted him to put his life on hold for her. She first became ill when he left for university, and she had told him not to abandon his aspirations for her – not that his younger brother or sister had necessarily agreed. They had stopped talking to him when he refused to return home.

But he knew his mum wouldn't want him to come home.

Still, he could hear Luke's voice saying, *who gives a shit, you come home anyway 'cause it's our mum.*

And Gray's response: *unfortunately, we can't all get by on weed dealing.*

The bus took him past familiar fields and he could still see him and Luke there, as kids, playing football. He could see through the window of his old classroom as he passed his old school, and he could see the bar they were kicked out of because Luke started a fight.

An overwhelming mixture of nostalgia and dread cascaded down his body. The pit of his stomach shook, his chest tightened.

Why did he feel so bad?

Why was this making him so nervous?

He'd done nothing wrong.

The tree on the corner of the estate came into view and he pressed the button that indicated to the driver he wished to get off. It was the same tree he'd climbed up and fallen off at eight-years-old.

He passed the same neighbours, albeit, they looked a little older, and it took a doubletake for them to realise who was looking at them. They all smiled and waved as they did, though.

It was probably the best reaction he was going to get.

He reached the house and realised he didn't have a key. He tried the door but it was locked. He knocked on it, but no one responded.

"Mum!" he shouted, though no noise responded to him.

Why wasn't she answering the door?

He walked around the back and opened the side-gate into the garden. Mum had never locked the backdoor, maybe he could get in that way.

He tried it, but it didn't budge.

He could see her, though. Inside the living room. Sat in a chair, motionless, her mouth wide and her eyes closed. She looked so... empty. Dormant. Like a doll flopped in a chair.

He banged on the window.

"Mum!"

She didn't wake up.

He put his hands on the window and pressed his nose against it so he could see better.

What he saw stiffened him.

Was that Mum?

How the hell did she look like that?

She was just skin and rags. Pale. Lifeless.

She was nothing of the vibrant woman ready to kick cancer in the butt that she was when he'd left.

Maybe he should have come home for a summer instead of staying at his girlfriend's.

The sound of the front door opening and closing wasn't enough to stir her. A familiar person walked through, his tracksuit bottoms and plain t-shirt and his tattooed hands and baggy eyes the same as they were three years ago.

Luke pressed a hand against Mum's forehead, his palm then the back of his hand.

Gray couldn't decide: should he make his presence known? Should he hide?

Then what?

He couldn't hide forever.

He banged on the window.

Luke looked up. His face curled, twisting and morphing and writhing and contorting into aggression.

"What the *fuck* are you doing here?" Luke demanded.

"Luke, please, just let me in."

"Let you in?"

"Come on, I've come home to see Mum. To see you."

Luke looked back, his face a conflict of reactions. He looked unsure whether to open the door or smash it down.

"Please, Luke," Gray said. "I'm sorry."

WHEN ARRIVING HOME, AMBER HAD EXPECTED TO FIND HER mother, asleep again, her head lolling to one side.

She expected to find emptiness.

She expected to find silence.

This was far from what she found.

"I was trying to do something better for myself!"

"And you couldn't wait until after she died!"

"It's not what she would have wanted!"

"But it's still what's right you soddin' bellend!"

The shouting voices halted at the sight of Amber entering the room. She looked upon red faces of Luke and Gray, head to head, Gray towering over Luke like he always had.

The two of them were the definition of contrast. Luke with his tattooed arms, tracksuit and t-shirt, greased up hair – standing opposite Gray, a sweatshirt over a shirt, hair parted to the side, his voice sounding just like someone who had returned from three years of university.

And, behind them, their mum.

Her head laid on her shoulder, but her eyes were open. Which was unusual, but even though they were open, they were empty. Yet, behind that emptiness, she could see what was hidden, and it looked like shame.

She looked between them, hands on her hips, biting her lip.

"You had to do this with her there, didn't you?" she said to both of them. Barging past them, she reached her mum's side and lifted her head, holding it up. Mum's eyes lifted to Amber's. They were tired, weak even.

"We didn't mean to-" Gray went to object.

"Shut up!" Amber snapped, surprising herself at her hostility. "This is the only day this week I have come home to find her not asleep. I wonder what was keeping her awake, huh?"

"This lanky prick started it," Luke blurted.

"Oh, lanky, what a smart insult, you degenerate little-"

"Enough!" Amber snapped once more. "I have to get her to the hospital."

"I thought that was yesterday," Luke said.

"It was. We have another one today."

"Oh, Amber, I keep saying-"

"This is the last one. And it's different."

"How?"

"I've gone private."

Luke stumbled over a few words before he finally managed to speak.

"How the hell did you afford that?"

Amber looked Luke up and down. For all the grief Luke had given Gray, he still lived on his friend's sofa and never gave any of his drug dealing money to the cause.

Probably because he spent it all on more weed.

"I spent the last of my savings."

"Oh, Amber, you shouldn't-"

"Well we were hardly going to use your savings, were we?"

"That ain't fair."

"Fair?" Amber put a cushion behind her mum's head and

paced toward the other two. "What about this is fair? Huh? What?"

Luke sighed and reluctantly nodded.

"Sorry, sis'."

Amber turned to Gray and looked him up and down. He looked so... healthy. So educated. It made her sick.

"And what's your excuse?" Amber demanded.

"What do you mean?"

"Why are you here?"

"I've finished uni, I thought I'd come back to see you. To see mum. Even to see this knob."

Amber didn't know what to say. She didn't blame him for going to find a better life, but she did blame him for his absence, however contradictory that may be.

"We need to set off now anyway," Amber said. "It's three bus stops."

"It's fine, I'll take you," Luke volunteered.

"Yeah?"

"I was going to go out with Mikey, but this is more important."

"I'll come," Gray spoke, his voice a mixture of fear and assertiveness.

"You what?" Luke began to object.

"Enough," Amber said. "If he wants to come, he can. Wherever he's been, it's his mum too."

This gave them enough time to have tea. Amber managed to find a way to make two cans of beans and half a loaf of bread from the freezer into a few plates of beans on toast.

She could feel Gray's disgust at the meal, but he kept quiet. She was ready to get really mad if he didn't. She asked him about university, about his friends, his course, his plans for teacher training – the whole time, feeling the heat from Luke on the other side of her.

By the time Gray had turned to Luke and said, "So what

49

have you been up to while I've been gone?" Luke was ready to snap.

Amber placed a hand on his wrist and squeezed it gently, and he stayed calm, and he spoke through gritted teeth.

"Not much. Just this and that, you know. Same old."

And that was the extent of the conversation.

The car ride to the hospital was much the same. Awkward silence. The only real conversation was either between Luke and Amber, or Gray and Amber. Gray attempted a few questions at Luke, but he either grunted a short answer or turned up the radio.

As much as she had disliked the silence up to now, she was grateful for it as they sat in the waiting room.

Their mum, the one thing they all had in common, was going through all those tests as they just sat there and waited.

Waited for the final confirmation that there was no chance.

After almost two long hours – about an hour and twenty minutes longer than any other doctor had ever taken – a secretary came out and called their name.

A secretary, not the doctor.

"Elsie Michaels?"

"That's us," Amber answered.

"You will be in room three with Doctor William Chesser. Would you like any water or coffee or anything before you go in?"

Water and coffee before finding out your mum is going to die.

Now she knew she was in private.

"No, we're fine," Amber said.

"Right then," the secretary responded, with a smile a little too big for her face. "If you'd like to follow me."

And as Amber walked, followed by her two brothers, she finally understood what was meant when a priest talked about walking through the valley of death.

THEY SAT IN THE THREE CHAIRS BEFORE THE DESK LIKE A BAD panel on a talent show. Amber, as ever, in the middle, Luke to her left and Gray to her right.

Doctor William Chesser sat opposite them, clear skin and gleaming smile. Even his white jacket made him look good. His hair was slicked back, his demeanour deliberate and confident, and everything about the way he spoke was somehow reassuring.

Looking around his office, Amber saw lots of framed certificates of his qualifications – but, unlike the last office she was in, there were no pictures of family placed between them.

"My name is Doctor William Chesser," he said, "But please, you can call me Will. How are we all today?"

Amber looked to her brothers either side of her. She'd never been asked this by a doctor before. Normally it was straight to the terminal illness or ramblings about how she needed support – no one had ever actually directly looked at her and asked, *how are you?*

She knew Will was asking all of them, but she also knew her gormless brothers expected her to be the one who interacted.

"Okay," she spoke uncertainly.

"Well, if you are doing okay," Will said, his voice like he was speaking in an advert, "Then fair play to you. In fact, if you are doing okay, then that is amazing. But I have a sneaking suspicion that you are not."

"Well, you know…"

"Yes, it isn't easy. Terminal illness is horrific to experience first-hand, but it's also horrific to experience in someone you love."

"I guess…"

"Your mother must be an amazing woman to inspire such love. And, even if she doesn't say it, she must be very proud of her children for fighting so hard for her."

She felt herself unwillingly gushing. His charm made him all the more endearing and she felt, even if only for a moment, that someone actually, finally, understood her.

He took her lack of response as a response in itself and smiled, clicking the lid of his pen as he readjusted position.

"So, I suspect you want to know what we could do for your mother."

"Yes please."

"Have you been to any other doctors before us?"

"Yes. You are the fifth."

He pursed his lips, narrowed his eyebrows, and sucked in a breath to indicate his understanding of what a horrible situation that must be.

"Fifth in how long?" he asked.

"About six weeks."

"Jeeze. No wonder it's been tough. You seem like you're really doing all you can."

She looked to her brothers, whose eyes were directed at their feet, as if they were feeling shameful that they weren't the ones to be trying so hard; at least that's what she assumed.

She nodded at the doctor.

"Well, I'll cut to the chase then. As I'm sure you've already been told four times, there is little to nothing that can be done for her medically."

Amber let a breath go she wasn't aware she was holding and dropped her head.

"Her body is shutting down, it's spread throughout her – another aggressive round of chemotherapy would only exacerbate things."

She gave an unwilling nod.

"But I'm sure you've already been told that."

"Yes. Yes, I have."

Life drained out of her.

Her last hope diminished. The flicker of optimism burnt out and faded into smoke.

"There is, however, one thing that we can try."

She didn't react, at first. She assumed he had just given her another sentence about her mum's awful condition.

Then the words registered, and she promptly lifted her head.

"What?" she asked, feeling her brothers' heads lift too.

Will clicked his pen a few more times, taking a moment of thought, then took a leaflet from his drawer. He opened the leaflet on the table and leant toward them. Without having any idea of the relevance to this leaflet, she leant forward to peer over it.

"Have you heard of a drug called Coloperol?"

"No."

"Well, I imagine you wouldn't. It's not been taken to market yet. It's still in the early stages, but it's a very promising drug, one that the medical community is very excited about."

"You think this drug could help?"

He stroked his chin and considered this for a moment.

"There is a medical trial in two weeks' time. They are

looking for subjects with a condition similar to your mother's. She could be a good candidate to try this drug."

She sat on the edge of her seat, her leg bouncing, hands flexing over her legs, practically giddy with excitement.

"We couldn't promise anything, of course, but I think it could be the best hope she has."

"Well, yes, of course!" she said, her words a mess, practically unable to contain her excitement. "Yes! Let's do it!"

"There is a cost, of course," Will said.

Ah.

A cost.

Of course.

Screw it.

Whatever it was, they'd find it, they'd scrimp and save and do whatever it took, they would find the money and they would pay it.

Yes.

This is it.

By God this is it.

She looked at her brothers beside her. Both sat forward, smiles burdening their faces, weakly creeping up on their previously feeble dispositions.

Her mum could be saved.

Their mum could be saved.

"We'll do it," Amber insisted. "Whatever the cost."

Luke could find a few hundred from dealing. Gray could find a few hundred from a summer job. She could get a few hundred from doing a few extra shifts.

They could manage it, surely.

"How much is it?" Amber asked.

"It is thirteen thousand pounds."

Amber's leg stopped bouncing. Her hands stopped flexing, and her excitement ended like it had been executed.

"Thirteen thousand?" she repeated, her voice a whisper without an echo.

And, just like that, the temporary hope she felt was gone.

And the realisation that her mum was going to die due to money set on her like a potent stench she could never shake off.

A FEW SEARCHES ON HER PHONE AND AMBER COULD ALREADY SEE what people were saying about Coloperol.

This is a revolutionary drug!

Ridded my mother of cancer.

Once they get this drug right it's going to change everything...

Could it really be that good?

These weren't just medical professionals saying this – it was people who'd been through the previous drug trials or known people who had.

What would be the chances it would save her mum?

Hell, if the chance was even one percent, she'd take it. But it seemed like the chance would be far greater than that.

Revolutionary. Ridded of cancer. Change everything.

She closed her eyes and ran her hands through her hair. Shaking her head. Willing the money to just appear. Willing it to just magically snap into physical form.

Is there a God? Doesn't he perform miracles?

If he did exist, the money would appear. Surely. No one would make a young, hopeful eighteen-year-old woman endure this.

She opened her eyes.

Nothing but leaflets about mortgages and savings.

"Miss Amber Michaels?"

"That's me," she said, picking up her bag and meeting the banker's open hand with hers.

"My name is Clifton, it's lovely to meet you. Right this way."

He guided her to a computer cordoned off from the other computers and indicated the chair opposite himself to Amber. She took it, leaning forward, hands on her lap, trying not to be too hopeful.

Trying.

Really trying.

"I understand you are here to talk about a bank loan, is that correct?"

"Yes, yes it is."

"May I ask what the loan is for?" asked Clifton, clicking the mouse, not averting his eyes from the monitor.

She wondered whether to tell the truth.

Then she wondered why she wouldn't.

"Medical bills," she said. "My mum's. She's sick, and we are trying to get her into a drug trial."

"Oh, I'm sorry to hear that," he said, still not taking his eyes from the screen. "And how much are you looking to borrow?"

"Thirteen thousand."

"Okay, let me just take a few details."

She told him where she lived, how much she earned and where she worked – a slight flicker on his face as she did. Just like everyone, she presumed that he thought she was a stripper, and she didn't bother to correct him.

Strippers make big tips, and maybe that would help, as if the more money she potentially made the more likely she would be to acquire the loan.

"Okay, let's see what the computer says then," he said, clicking a final icon and awaiting the computer's verdict.

Unable to see the screen, she watched him intently, hand curled in front of her mouth, waiting, just waiting, a seemingly meaningless decision to the bank that could decide whether someone lives or dies.

"Okay," Clifton said, clicking the mouse a few more times.

She wished he would just tell her.

Then she wished he hadn't.

"I'm afraid the bank is unable to give you a loan at this time," he stated.

She ran through his statement numerous times in her mind to make sure she'd understood, to see if there was any way she could have misconstrued, that he hadn't meant what she was sure he had.

"Can I ask why not?"

"Your income does not reflect what you can pay back. If you wanted to try for a lower loan, then we could try that."

"How much?"

"I imagine, say, three thousand?"

She scoffed. Covered her head with her hand.

She didn't want to take anything out on this man, but she hated how little he cared.

"Thanks for your time," she grunted, getting up and leaving before she said anything she would probably not regret.

She stepped into the street. It was raining, and quite heavily. She hadn't an umbrella, but it didn't matter. She could get wet. The rain could drench every part of her for all she cared.

Then she saw it. That same Mercedes, driving down the street with its engine roaring and its speed excessive.

Soaking another load of unexpecting innocent members of the public at the bus stop.

She tried to catch a glimpse of the driver, but the windows were blacked out. She wasn't even able to get a silhouette.

She trudged home, thinking of nothing but the bank and the Mercedes.

The arseholes who wouldn't give her the money, and the arsehole who had too much.

Just as she thought it, an idea crept upon her.

No.

Stupid idea.

Stupid, stupid idea.

She could end up in prison. They all could.

Then again, did she care?

In prison with her mum alive, or out of prison standing by a grave?

No question at all.

She arrived home to find Luke and Gray in the living room. Luke was helping their mum finish a yoghurt whilst Gray sat on the sofa, watching.

Neither of them spoke.

"Hey, Luke," she said, "could I talk to you in the kitchen?"

He looked to her, to the yoghurt, to their mum and back at Amber.

"Sure," he said.

"I'll take it," Gray offered, taking the yoghurt reluctantly handed over by Luke.

Luke followed Amber, glancing over his shoulder at Gray, feeling a little resentful, but quietly pleased that he was doing something to help.

Once they were in the kitchen, Amber shut the door and looked at him, nervously biting her lip.

"What is it?" Luke asked, looking concerned.

"I just had a question," Amber mused, "and I wondered if you might know the answer."

"Oh yeah, what's that?"

Amber couldn't help it. She felt her face twist into conniving, sneaky smirk, a look that announced that she was up to something, a look that announced the initial thoughts of a wicked plan.

"I was just wondering," she said, "how easy it would be to rob a house?"

PART III

YOU WANT TO DO WHAT?

Sheila Hamsmith was yesterday's news.

The press was still yapping on about it, yes, but for him – she was done.

Dusted. Mutilated. Violated. Dead.

Now it was time to dispose of the body.

Unfortunately, this was posing him quite the dilemma. He'd previously had two pigs that he kept on his land – far enough from his back entrance that he didn't have to smell them, close enough that he didn't have to lug a body too far.

Pigs are glorious creatures.

Not for petting or loving or anything, of course.

But for eating.

For example, did you know that pigs will eat every single part of a human body?

They will eat *anything*.

He wasn't quite sure how he'd known this when he came up with the genius idea a few months ago, but he was glad he had. Those two pigs he bought were the best investment he'd ever made – they disposed of every inch of evidence.

But those two pigs died.

It was an unfortunate accident, really.

He couldn't be bothered to go out and find a woman to kill, so pigs were the next best thing.

Besides, kill a woman and you can't have bacon the next morning.

Come to think of it, why was he growing such a particular penchant for women?

There was a time when he catered for men – not sexually, not in that way, but more in his morbid fascination. He was curious as to what would happen if you walked up to someone who pissed you off and kept beating them and beating them and beating them until they went limp – then kept beating some more.

In fact, the first person he'd killed was a man. Once he'd decided he wanted to murder someone, he'd had to choose who to murder.

That was when he'd searched for Jasper Pearson on Facebook.

He still held onto a memory of being fourteen-years-old, braces fixed to his teeth, and being pantsed repeatedly by Jasper Pearson – the boy whose parents had so much money that their last name was on a metal plaque outside the private school they both attended.

There were a few pictures of Jasper Pearson on Facebook, outside his new home, with a street sign in the distance – one that really had to be zoomed in on to read – and a house number behind Jasper's smug tosspot face.

Jasper had been almost too easy to find, which had made the murder less satisfying than he'd hoped...

Anyway.

Enough about Jasper. He'd long since been digested.

Back to the pigs.

He was hesitant to just google *how to buy pigs* – as, surely, if someone was to check up on his internet history, they would come across this and consider it to be suspicious. It was almost as bad as googling *how do I get rid of a body?*

He readied a reason in case he needed it. He had a lot of land, so much so he'd had to employ a full-time gardener. He could quite easily say he'd decided to use some of it for farming.

Yes, farming.

Perfect.

Not for disposing of the remains of his fetish for mutilation.

A gurgle stopped him from his thoughts. Eve had woken up, and she was just beginning to realise she was bound by rope.

Eve was the perfect victim, really, as she was a prostitute. Not that he ever felt guilty about killing someone, but he felt even more not guilty when killing a sex worker.

After all, it's what they are there for, isn't it?

She began screaming.

He had a migraine coming.

He picked up a mallet, lifted it back, and swung it into her face and left it there, wedged between her newly loosened eye and collapsing teeth.

She stopped screaming, and he was finally able to return to his computer.

His first results showed him how to purchase something called a micro pig. It appeared that a new fad had arrived where people were buying micro pigs for pets. This was both pathetic and useless.

Pathetic – as why would you have food as a pet?

Useless – as a pig that size would never be able to digest Eve.

Eve was a slender, beautiful woman, yes – but a pig that size would still get full way too soon.

No, best keep looking.

He narrowed down his search.

Buy pigs online.

A site offering pigs to be rehomed, a site called *Preloved,* appeared first. The site name made him gag.

Another result appeared: *suckling pigs online.*

He gagged once more, then realised he'd read it incorrectly.

He redefined his search again, beginning to find it tiresome, but thinking he could hardly allocate his secretary this task without the nosy little bitch asking irritating questions.

Adopt pigs for farm.

The RSPCA came up first.

He threw the computer across the room, taking delight in the smashing of the screen against the far wall, its bits and pieces falling over Eve's static face like metal rain.

Fuck it, he'd just get acid instead.

How long does a body take to dissolve in acid?

He laughed. He could hardly google that…

Screw it, Sheila and Eve would be fine in this room for now.

Actually, no.

Sheila was beginning to stink.

"Finnnnnnnne!" he moaned to himself.

He'd go to the RSPCA and apply to adopt a pig. Hopefully he could have one within a few days.

He sighed as he picked up his car keys.

He really didn't want to speak to the RSPCA.

He fucking hated vegetarians.

GRAY WAS THE ONE WHO NEEDED CONVINCING.

Luke tried to insist they didn't need him – but Amber was stubborn in her decision. If they were going to do this, they were going to do it together.

The first conversation went just as Amber had expected.

"Are you guys insane?" Gray had protested. "You want to rob a guy's house! You do know that's breaking the law, right?"

"I told you," Luke had knowingly said to Amber, which wasn't helpful.

"If you can find another way..."

"I will," Gray protested. "I will find another way!"

"We don't have much time."

"Give me until tonight, and I'll find a way."

She'd had no choice.

Even though she knew what would happen, she had to let him try it. Frustrating, yes, but she would be the same.

They both had too much of their mum in them.

So he'd been to the bank – in fact, he'd been to four. Then, he'd been to the valuables exchange to see what they'd give for their most invaluable of valuables. He'd then spend the rest of his afternoon ringing around local businesses, explaining the situation, and seeing what money they could raise.

Now it was tonight, and Amber had never seen Gray go from so smartly put together to so dishevelled in such a short time. They sat around the kitchen table, the low wattage light above doing little to endow the room with light. Luke sat back in his chair, one hand leisurely draped over its back and the other on the table with a cigarette pressed between his fingers.

Amber sat forward, her hands together.

And Gray, well... Gray sat with his shirt poking out of his trousers and his hair in ungroomed tufts. An image she hadn't seen of Gray in a long while.

Then again, she hadn't spent this much time with Gray in a long while.

"Had a busy day?" Luke asked sarcastically and did all he could not to begin his cocky chuckle.

Amber couldn't help but smile. She could see him suffering the exasperation she'd been suffering while he was away. It was strange, but, for a moment, it made her feel less alone.

"It's..." Gray tried. "It's impossible. There's nothing. No one wants to help. It's like no one cares."

"Wow," Luke said, shaking his head. "You really don't live in this world, do you, mate?"

"Would you quit it?"

"How about both of you quit it," Amber interjected. "Gray, what's it going to be? We need a decision."

Empty silence followed.

Amber and Luke stared at Gray, waiting for a response that didn't come.

Until, eventually, it did.

"Say we were going to do this," Gray said. "How would we do it?"

Amber looked to Luke. He was the one with the limited

criminal experience, and she was about to find out just how limited that experience was.

"The whole thing should take no more than thirty minutes," Luke said, quickly and astutely. "We get in, eliminate the variables, then get out."

"The variables?" Gray repeated.

"Things that could go wrong. Example – the guy who lives there. If his car is home, first thing we need to do is locate him."

"And do what with him?"

"If you let me finish." Luke lifted a hand and waited for silence, then stretched out the silence to make a point. "It's a big house. If the geezer's in there, we could easily wander around without ever bumping into him. I will locate him and either make sure we avoid that part of the house, or do whatever we need to keep him quiet."

"What does keep him quiet mean?"

"Some things you're better off not knowing. I'll also need to dismantle the alarm once we're in, which is fine."

"How on earth are you going to do that?"

"Leave it to me. Once that's all done, it leaves us time to get in, fill our bags, and get out."

"My only issue," Gray said, all of them knowing he had far from one single issue, "is that, if he is so rich and the house is so big, he's bound to have more security than just alarms. Like, CCTV or something."

"We wear masks until we're sure."

"And I'm not so sure about you sorting him out..."

"Fine! Option B – we go there and wait."

"Wait for what?"

"For father fucking Christmas to arrive, what do you think? Until we see him leave."

Amber found her arms shaking. She filled with doubt, questions firing back and forth, her mind changing again and again.

She only had to think of Mum in the next room to quell those doubts.

"But – what about this guy we're going to rob?" Gray asked.

"He's an arsehole," Amber said. "Trust me."

"You know him?"

"We've seen him in town, soaking pedestrians and speeding around in his Mercedes."

"And what if we get caught?"

"So what?"

"We go to prison."

"We get a year, maybe two. Then we come out and our mum is alive."

Gray flinched.

"She'd do the same for us," Amber claimed.

Gray nodded, a nod that turned more vigorous.

"Okay. Okay, right. Say we do this, say we go through with this – this preposterous idea – when? When would we do it?"

Amber looked from Luke to Gray, to Luke, back to Gray again.

She hadn't thought about when, but it took three decisive seconds for her to answer.

"Tonight," she said. "We do it tonight."

16

Amber's afternoon was mostly taken up by pacing from one end of a room to another, staring at the window as if she was waiting for something, and changing her mind back and forth as much as her indecisive thoughts would allow her to.

Whenever she needed reassurance that she was doing the right thing, that this was their only choice, that they *had* to do it; whenever her doubts began to overwhelm her – she sat by her mum for five minutes.

And, as if written in fate, beside her mum was where she found herself at five minutes to five, just as the dark winter evening was settling in and it was precisely five minutes before they would leave.

Then something happened – something she had not expected. Something that rarely ever happened, especially not in the afternoon when it would be time for Mum to nap.

Mum spoke to her.

"Hello, dear," she said, so feebly yet so casually, as if nothing had ever happened, as if it was just them talking about her day at school or their weekend plans.

"Mum?" Amber said, taken aback, hearing a voice she hadn't heard in weeks, almost months.

"How was..." her voice faded away, about to ask a question but not having the strength to finish it.

Amber took both of her mum's cold, clammy hands in hers.

"What is it, Mum?" she tried.

A vacant expression gazed back at her.

"You were about to say something, what was it?"

An empty face. Drooping eyes. Head dropping to the shoulder.

"Come on, Mum, what was it? How was what?"

Mum's eyes closed.

Amber dropped her head, keeping her hands in each of Mum's.

Tears shivered in the base of Amber's eyes. She closed her eyes tight in an attempt to stop them, but her quivering lip was enough to stop her resisting.

She took her hands from her mum's and put them over her face.

If either of her brothers walked in, she did not want them to see her like this.

Amber closed her eyes and she was twelve again. Dumped by a boy she had a crush on when he refused to hold her hand.

Such a ridiculous thing for a twelve-year-old to be upset about. Now she was older, she could never understand why she was in such a rush to 'go out' with a boy, and why she didn't just enjoy being a child.

Nevertheless, she had been inconsolable.

Her dad had told her to stop it, she was just a kid. Neither of her brothers were interested, being stroppy, acne-ridden teenagers themselves. All of her friends were too young to understand.

But Mum...

She had placed her arms neatly around Amber as she sat on

her lap and held her so tight Amber didn't care if she could breathe. She had snuggled into her mother's jumper, feeling it getting wetter and wetter, but not once did her mum care or object.

Her mum had just held her.

Not saying a word. No advice. No attempt at reassurance. As if she knew there was nothing to be said in such a moment, that nothing could quell heartache, no succinctly crafted sentences could logicise this to being okay.

She just allowed Amber to cry, with warm arms letting Amber know she was there.

Now, on her knees and doing all she could to restrain her tears, Amber would give anything for her mum to just reach out, hold her against her jumper, and know that not a word was needed to be said.

As it was, a gentle snore pushed through Mum's dry lips. The only evidence she was alive.

Amber shook her head. She couldn't let her brothers see her like this.

She stood, moving away from Mum to a box of tissues, and sorted herself out.

She leant against the fireplace, one hand in her hair that suddenly felt so sweaty, the other propping her chin up.

"You okay?" came Gray's voice.

She knew she had red eyes and a red face. She dried her eyes and blew her nose one last time.

"I'm fine," she said, turning around and feeling Gray's wary stare – a look on his face that showed he hadn't a clue what to say to help her. She suddenly felt as distant from him as she had ever been.

"Are you sure, because–"

"I said I'm fine."

Amber knew she had snapped but didn't care. She didn't want to talk.

"It's time to go," said Luke, appearing behind Gray.

She nodded and forced a smile.

Luke didn't ask her if she was okay. He could see she wasn't. He just gave a simple smile back.

With a glance back at Mum, Amber followed the others out of the house and to the car.

17

THE CAR WAS FILLED WITH CONTENT SILENCE.

Amber wished she had her phone. Normally, at times like this, she would be procrastinating on social media, or playing another round of WordBubble. But Luke had been pretty clear – they were to leave their mobile phones at home in order to avoid leaving history of their route via their phones' GPS; something that had put one of his friends in prison.

So they continued in silence, idol hands stretching and tapping and twisting.

It was a far better silence than Amber had been used to – it wasn't silence of friction or anger or hostility between her brothers, but rather a silence of nerves and trepidation. Despite no one voicing it, she knew everyone was thinking the same thing:

What are we doing?

Luke did pretty well to remember the drive considering how angry he'd been the first time he did it. He pulled the car over around a hundred yards from the gates and turned the engine off. No one went to get out.

"What if one of these other houses sees us?" Gray asked.

Luke looked around at the other houses, hidden up large drives far beyond their gates. It was as if the richer they were, the further from the street they were.

"Unless they have a telescope, it's unlikely," Luke answered.

"So what do we do now?" Amber asked.

"We wait."

"For what?"

"Until we see his Mercedes either coming or going. Something that lets us know if he's in or not." He opened the drop down and took out a share bag of Starbursts. "Sweet?"

Amber didn't think she could eat anything. Her stomach was still churning over what little tea she'd managed to push down, stuck somewhere between feeling sick and feeling hungry.

"No, thanks," she replied.

He turned and offered one to Gray who shook his head.

"Fine," Luke decided. "More for me."

He took out a strawberry Starburst. Amber knew this was his favourite from all those car rides as children where they'd have Starbursts and he'd only eat the red ones, leaving the rest to Amber.

She abruptly realised she would never get those days back. Childhood was over. Monotonous days of adulting had begun.

They only had to wait twenty minutes until Luke broke everyone's day dreams by saying, "Heads up."

The gates opened and the Mercedes drove out. As it drove past them, they all tried to peer through the window to see the owner, but the blacked-out windows remained in their way.

"Now's the time," Luke said. He took a plastic bag from beneath his chair and handed each of them a balaclava.

Amber took hers and looked at it, considering the cliché of it. A bunch of thieves in balaclavas, like in a bad movie.

She placed it on and looked at the other two. She could still see Gray's fear despite his face being covered.

Looking at the other two, it suddenly felt so real.

She filled with nerves, the kind of panic you get just before you go on stage or enter a job interview – that kind of panic when you decide to go back, to not go through with the performance, and have to force yourself forward.

Luke took a pen knife from the drop down and put it in his pocket.

"What's that for?" Amber gasped. "We're not going to hurt anyone!"

He opened the car door.

"Wait!" interrupted Gray. "Should we just – I don't know – should we think about this?"

"Thinking time's over, Gray. Time to save mum."

Luke left the car.

Amber looked over her shoulder at Gray. She knew how he felt.

Despite that, she opened her car door and stood out.

Finally, he followed.

They ran to the gate, Luke leading them. He shook the gate to feel its sturdiness, then turned to the other two.

"Watch what I do," he instructed.

He placed his hands on the bars, then held tightly as he placed the soles of his feet on the bars too. Like a monkey, he shimmied his way upwards, and jumped over the top.

"Now your turn," he said.

Amber took hold of the bars and tried to press her feet against them. Her body hung lower than Luke's had, and her feet slipped, but she kept grip.

"That's fine, you're doing fine," Luke assured her.

In a quick scurry, she made her way over the gate and jumped down.

"Your turn."

Gray looked over his shoulders, not just looking down the street but peering into far windows, too far back to see anyone, wondering if someone was watching and calling the police right now.

"Hurry up," Luke urged him.

With a sigh, Gray grabbed hold of the bars and awkwardly shimmied up, leapt over the side and collapsed onto his back.

"You're pathetic," Luke said, turning and sauntering across the drive.

Gray went to charge at Luke but Amber put a hand across him.

"Not now," she said.

Luke waved them over to the side of the driveway where they were in the shadows of trees. It took them a few minutes to make their way to the house, but once they saw it, they couldn't help but stand back and marvel.

It was bigger than they could have imagined. Old-fashioned stone and brick, with at least five floors, and wide enough to fit their house five or six times. The windows were pressed inwards, the front door black and grand, with a huge surrounding garden cordoned off by impressively sculpted bushes.

"This way," Luke whispered, waving the others to follow. He made his way across the side of the house and into the garden, where the guy's land went far into the distance.

This is unreal, Amber thought.

She glanced at Gray to see what he was thinking, but the balaclava kept his reaction hidden.

They reached the back door. Luke took out a hammer and looked to his left, to his right, then at the others.

"We sure about this?" he asked. "After this point, there's no turning back."

Amber wanted to object. As did Gray.

But neither of them did.

That was good enough for Luke. He smashed the window embedded in the back door, reached his arm through and grabbed hold of the door handle. He appeared to the other two to struggle with something, then the door pushed open.

"Wait here," he instructed.

Beeps sounded – pre-noise to the defeaning screech of an alarm.

Amber tensed herself, ready to run, ready to abort.

Then Luke took out a small utensil, rushed inside and, searching the kitchen cupboards, found the alarm box on his fourth attempt.

The beeps grew more frequent.

"Luke…" Amber urged.

He ignored her, too full of concentration for the voice of inexperience. He attached two wires from his contraption to the alarm and watched a small screen.

Although she had no idea what the gadget was, she knew exactly how it worked, and was impressed – then felt bad for feeling impressed, for entertaining the notion that Luke's knowledge of criminal technology was something to be proud of.

"Come on, come on, come on," Luke urged.

Too late. The alarm wailed.

But, within two seconds of the alarm starting, Luke saw something on the screen – and he used whatever it was he saw to jab a few buttons on the alarm box.

The alarm ended.

He put the contraption back into his pocket and turned to the others.

"You coming in or what?"

They stepped across the threshold and closed the door behind them.

They were in.

18

Even the kitchen was unbelievable. It was like a perfectly gelled mixture of classic and modern interior. A glass table to eat at, but with a classical stove. The juxtaposition somehow worked, somehow made it even fancier.

Amber stopped admiring. She didn't have time to stand back and gape at a room that was probably more expensive than the whole of her house. She had a job to do.

They had a job to do.

"This way," Luke whispered. He led them through another few rooms, past a wall of hanging grand paintings in gold frames, some that Amber recognised from studying Art GCSE, to a set of stairs that looked like they belonged on Titanic.

Luke stopped at a large grandfather clock beside a lift door and turned to the others.

"We start from the top, work our way down," Luke told Amber. "I go left, you go right, then we meet back in the middle. We go to down to the next floor, then the next, then the next, 'til we have enough."

"What do I do?" Gray asked.

"You stay here, watch the front door," Luke instructed.

"If you see his car or hear the front door key unlock, make this clock go off then get out the back and meet us there."

Gray nodded. He wouldn't like that Luke only deemed him competent of 'lookout' – but Amber was sure Gray was secretly pleased that he had such a simple job.

"Ready?" Luke asked.

Amber vaguely nodded.

Luke shuffled into the lift, Amber next to him. She was curious to see how far the buttons went. Luke hit the highest number – floor six.

Finally stood still, Amber could now feel the thumping of her heart against her chest, punching against her ribs like a bird fighting against its cage.

"You okay?" Luke asked, noticing her hands clutching onto the rails.

She caught sight of herself in the mirror, forgetting she was wearing the balaclava. She terrified herself.

"Yeah," she answered, not realising how out of breath she was until she spoke.

"Cool it," Luke urged, his voice so calm and smooth. "You're doing fine."

"I know... I just..." She went to wipe perspiration from her brow, again forgetting about the balaclava.

"We'll be in and out in no time. Honestly."

She nodded.

What else could she do?

Luke withdrew two bin bags that he'd stuffed into his back pocket and passed one to Amber.

She took the bin bag and stared at it, a black crumpled mess clutched inside her sweaty palm.

He removed his balaclava and nodded at Amber that she was now okay to remove hers.

"Just find anything that looks valuable that can fit in the bag and put it in. Sweep through, don't look too much, just whatever you see."

"Okay."

"Any cash or money you find, the better."

"Okay."

"And Amber?"

"Yeah?"

He extended a hand and placed it on her shoulder.

"Just remember we're doing this for Mum, yeah?"

She nodded.

She was glad he said that.

It allowed her to calm her breathing, to quell her raging heart, to cease her racing thoughts.

For Mum.

The doors pinged and opened.

around the others, wooden beams of brown and white holding up the ceiling.

Imagine a life where you get to live somewhere like this.

Thirteen thousand on an operation would mean very little. It probably wouldn't even make a dent on the bank balance.

How strange, what a sum of money can mean to one person compared to the other.

For the guy who owns this house, it would probably mean a good night out.

For them, it meant the life of their mum.

For a fleeting moment, guilt left him. He'd always resented people who resented the rich, as the rich were often rich because they had earnt it. They had the money they had because they'd worked day and night for it.

Unfortunately, it wasn't that simple.

Money pays for an education that leads to such work. It is too difficult to go between classes, and people are often condemned by the level of privilege they are born into.

He sighed.

What did it really matter?

He closed his eyes, just for a moment.

Listened to the ticking of the grandfather clock.

Tick.

Tick.

Tick.

Back and forth the pendulum swung.

A chime announced a new hour.

He sat up and buried his head in his arms, covered his face, exasperated from overthinking.

This was why he hadn't come home in the holidays. Because of the strife, the stress, the pointless going on and on about the choices he'd made, Luke had made, Amber had made.

He opened his mouth and pushed out a sigh.

A sigh that showed how he felt – but had an effect he had not intended.

This sigh was loud.

Perhaps, too loud.

Or, at least, loud enough to cover up the sound of an engine on the driveway.

THE CORRIDOR WAS DARK, BUT AMBER SUPPOSED IT HAD TO BE. Despite the house being far away from any prying eyes, her paranoia still told her that a light could attract attention from the outside. She had to do this in the shadows.

She began in a bedroom that appeared barely used. A disgusting floral duvet hugged the mattress, an ageing wooden cupboard stood ashamedly in the far corner, and a fancy dresser leant casually against the wall.

She opened the first drawer of the dresser and marvelled at a sight that did not look real.

Wow.

She wasn't sure if she'd ever seen this much variety of jewellery in her life. There were all kinds of gold: carved yellow, white, even rose. There was fine silver, diamond-encrusted silver, and all other kinds of silver too expensive for her to recognise. There was so much of it the drawer could barely contain its riches.

Does this person even know this is here?

Maybe he inherited this house.

Maybe he wasn't even aware these items existed.

In a house this big it would be quite easy to never go in some rooms for years, and end up losing track of possessions.

Would he even notice the jewellery was missing?

She took the drawer straight out of the dresser and turned it upside down into the bin bag. The bag, despite being far from full, grew heavier.

With that drawer gone, she saw the contents of another drawer beneath it, just as full. Rings, necklaces, bracelets, even a bloody diadem.

"Jackpot," she whispered to herself, feeling herself getting way too into this.

How much could all this go for?

Could they have enough in her bag already?

This was a genius idea.

She tipped the drawer into the bag and, finding the final drawer beneath it also full, she tipped that too.

She threw the bag over her shoulder as she trudged through the en suite and into the next corridor. The cheap quality bin bag was already breaking against the strain (what did she expect?) but she knew she didn't have to fill it with much more.

The corridor displayed a succession of doors on either side, leading to a corner with a large window. Glistening laminate floor led her path – probably cleaned thoroughly by someone else getting paid minimum wage.

She went to open the first door and found it was locked.

That was not going to deter her.

She took a run up and barged into the door.

Nothing.

She barged again.

And again.

Bemoaning her lack of strength, she gave up, and went to the next room – which happened to be unlocked. A desktop computer sat on a sturdy, pristine wooden desk, beside a vast amount of bookcases displaying titles such as *Against Nature*,

The Call of Cthulu and *The Complete Tales of Edgar Allen Poe*. Most bookcases were filled with fiction, though there was one bookcase full of texts on teaching theories.

Shit. Is this guy a teacher?

No, he couldn't be. He drove a Mercedes.

Thinking nothing of it, she grabbed the flat screen monitor and a few of the older looking books – they could be worth something – and took them into the corridor where her bin bag lay open for her.

Just as she finished piling the items into the ever-expanding bag, something caught her attention.

Something that made every hair on her body stick on end.

A flicker of light from outside the window.

With an air of caution, a caution she didn't particularly understand, she edged toward the window and peered at the drive below.

And, on that drive, was a Mercedes, slowing down and parking.

GRAY SHOOK HIMSELF OUT OF HIS FUNK.

Now wasn't the time to get all dark and depressed about life.

Now was the time to focus. To listen. To make sure...

What was that noise?

He rushed to the window. Something went by, but it went too fast, he only saw the end of it, what was it?

He listened intently.

What was that?

Was that an engine?

The sound of an engine dying and a car door opening answered his question.

"Shit!"

He'd been so busy wallowing he hadn't noticed.

Right, that was a car.

A car.

A car.

Dammit.

What now? What was he supposed to do?

He ran back and forth, trying to collect his thoughts, trying to distinguish between each piece of indeterminate panic floating around his mind.

What had Luke said? To warn them? How should he do that? What was the plan?

The grandfather clock.

He ran up to it. Looked it up and down. As tall as he was, but standing far more proudly.

What was he supposed to do?

Make it go. Make it go off.

Make the clock go off.

Right.

That's what he had to do.

Make it make a sound. Go off. An alarm or something.

Does a grandfather clock have an alarm?

No, it doesn't.

He reached his hands out to do what he was supposed to do – but how was he meant to do that?

How was he meant to make it make sound?

To *go off* as Luke had so eloquently put it?

He lifted the screen and took the handles in his fingers. He could move them easily.

He moved the handles to an hour. That would make it chime. It always chimed on the hour.

Chime.

That was it.

Just one chime.

One sodding chime.

That wasn't enough! They were on the top floor, they wouldn't hear that!

He bounced from one foot to the other.

He could go. He could run out the backdoor now, and he'd escape, uncaptured and unharmed.

Or I could fight the guy.

Hell, who was he kidding? He couldn't beat up a kitten. The

closest he'd come to a confrontation was when someone, by their own fault, spilt their pint on him, and he had apologised profusely to avoid getting punched.

He hit the side of the clock. Hit it again. Harder.

What was that meant to do?

Like the clock was going to make noise upon being assaulted?

He shifted his body.

From one foot to the other. To the other. To the other.

Oh, shit.

He had no idea how to make it make sound. He should have asked. Should have thought about this.

Fuck, he should have done a lot of things.

Footsteps on the gravel driveway grew closer.

He looked over his shoulder at the front door.

It didn't move. Or budge. Or falter.

Where was this guy going?

He tried opening the main body of the clock. It took a bit of a pull, but he managed.

All he found were cogs and whirs and a hundred things he didn't understand. He had a history degree, not engineering. He couldn't even mend a plug. He'd screw up putting a picture on the wall. What was he supposed to do with this?

He looked over his shoulder again.

He ran up a few steps and paused, gripping the bannister.

"Amber!"

Nothing.

"Luke!"

Nothing.

"Amber! Luke!"

He was barely even shouting.

He looked back at the door.

Screw it.

"Amber! Luke!" he screamed, so hard his voice broke under the strain.

No response.

It was too late.

It was all too late.

He rushed through the room, leaving the grandfather clock behind, through the corridor, back through the kitchen, to the backdoor.

The backdoor that opened.

The backdoor that opened and revealed a man,

The backdoor that opened and revealed a man with a large grin on his face, walking with a suave step and a suit to match.

"Hello," said the man. "What do we have here?"

22

Shit.

Shit shit shit.

Shit shit shit shit shit.

Amber didn't know what to do. She bounced from one wall to the other, running her hands through her hair, leaving them stuck in the solidity of her dried sweat.

She'd find Luke.

That's what she'd do.

She'd find Luke. Carry on around the corridor, find him.

She began to run, then halted.

The bag.

It had everything she needed to save Mum.

Whatever happened, she couldn't leave it.

She doubled back, picked it up, then carried on running around the corner.

She entered another new corridor, longer than the one before, to find two more corridors. She took one, to find another two corridors. She chose one, to find another three, then another two, until she stopped, suddenly aware that she was completely, unequivocally, totally lost.

She dropped the bag.

Stuck her hands in her hair.

Paced back and forth.

Should she go back on herself?

If she did, would she even know which way to go, or would she just be even more lost?

No, the best thing to do would be to go on.

She carried on walking, her legs feeling like they were filled with lead, like she was wading through water, like there were weights tied to her ankles.

She reached a dead end.

Just two doors, nothing else.

Maybe it was through one of those doors?

She listened. Tried to see if she could hear a car door opening, or, even better, a car driving away.

She listened.

Listened.

Listened.

Like she was going to hear anything this far up and this far in. She was in a labyrinth of undiscovered rooms.

She looked at the two doors. One of them would surely take her to the next corridor, or they'd be a throughway.

She should have just gone back on herself to start with. As it was, she had no choice but to shout.

"Luke?" she tried.

Maybe he was close by.

"Luke, are you there?"

She was going to have to shout louder.

If she wanted to stand a chance, she was going to have to raise her voice.

She closed her eyes, told herself she had no choice, that there was no way the guy would be this far up the house by now.

Maybe he wasn't even inside yet. She hadn't heard the

grandfather clock. He could have left.

Could he?

"Luke!" she wailed. Or, at least, she tried as much as her weary voice could let her.

Nothing but an eerie silence responded.

Fuck it.

She tried the door to her left. It took a bit of leveraging, being a bit stiff, but a good push forced the door to swing open.

Darkness returned her stare without disguise or fear.

She reached a hand out to the wall, searched for a light, but found none.

She searched the other side of the door.

She crept forward a few steps, reaching her arm out for something, anything, something that would guide her way. A chair, or a desk maybe.

Her foot kicked something.

She crouched, feeling her hand over whatever it was.

It felt stiff. Hard, yet soft. Something crusty.

A discarded plate, maybe.

She stepped over whatever it was and edged forward. Her outreaching hand touched a desk, and she grabbed hold of it. Searching the desk, she finally found a lamp.

She turned it on.

A gentle, orange-tinted illumination cast a small light over the room.

She looked at what she had just felt.

Eyes stared back at her.

Beside that, another set of eyes.

She recognised those eyes.

That girl... the news...

It took a couple of seconds to register that these faces were real. Empty, stiff – but real.

Once she did realise, she flattened herself up against the wall.

Screamed.

Screamed again.

Two blood-encrusted naked corpses lay upon the floor.

One of their heads was so bashed in that a wayward eye poked out, held on by a loose piece of artery.

The other's hair was crusted to the floor via a puddle of dried red gunk.

One of them was still on all fours, stuck like a dog, rigid as a doll.

Eventually, her thoughts reformed some resemblance of coherence.

This was a mistake.

She wondered if she'd make it out of this house alive.

PART IV

IN HERE WITH ME

He grinned a lecherous grin.

Looked like he wasn't going to have to venture out for his kill tonight.

No prowling the clubs.

No working on the right woman with the right hair and the right face and the right lipstick.

Not too much red, but a slight tinge.

Not too much perfume, but enough to excite him as they brushed past.

The stress over whether she was the right one. The worst thing that could happen is he'd choose the wrong one and have to go through all this for someone who wasn't worth it.

But not tonight.

Not needed.

Could wait.

Maybe another night.

He'd arrived home to a beautiful sight.

He had everything he needed right here.

GRAY'S FEET ITCHED. HE SWIVELLED BACK AND FORTH.

Should he run at this guy?

Or should he run from this guy?

But this guy was standing right in front of the backdoor, and he was standing so, so still. There was no shock or surprise, no fear in his face, no *holy shit I'm calling the police get out of my house* – just a smile, slanting upwards at the side of his mouth.

Gray could try to fight, though he was sure he'd be lousy at it. He would quite eagerly apologise to someone who had barged into him so that person didn't take offence to Gray's existence.

Maybe now was the time to start.

But he knew he couldn't. He wasn't even sure he knew how to throw a punch. And he doubted that, if he did, it would have much effect.

The guy didn't look particularly well-built. He was slim, but not muscular. Maybe that could work in Gray's favour?

But, even though he didn't look well-built, he still somehow looked powerful; the kind of man who would tread on Gray's family then wipe the remnants off his shoe.

The man took a step forward and Gray immediately echoed the step backwards.

Why couldn't Gray move any more than this? Why couldn't he just run and hide or run and escape? Why was he so frantically immobile?

The man chuckled at Gray's reaction.

"You look as white as a ghost," the man observed. Not in an aggressive, demeaning or hostile manner – more like he was talking to an old friend he hadn't seen in a while, like he was pleasantly surprised to see him.

Gray's mouth stuttered open but only a feeble murmur came out. Not only did the ability to move escape him, so did the ability to talk or shout.

That's what he should do.

Shout for the others.

Three on one and they'd be fine, right?

I mean, Luke knows how to handle himself...

Luke could take this guy out.

God, now I'm looking for my little brother to protect me...

No, Gray. Now's not the time.

Run. Fight. Do something for Christ's sake...

"What's your name?" the man asked.

Gray went to answer then stopped himself, dumbfounded by the casual question.

"I said, what is your name?"

"I– I– I'm not telling you."

The man nonchalantly shrugged.

"Fair enough," he said. "I'm knackered. I'm making a coffee, you want one?"

The man sauntered into his kitchen and opened the cupboard, taking out coffee. Not instant coffee granules or powder or the

Tesco value stuff Amber had been giving him since he'd arrived home – no, the man took out a packet of coffee beans, and began pouring them into the top of a rather fancy coffee machine.

Gray found himself absently floating into the kitchen, staying close to the door.

"You like it?" the man asked, noticing Gray's stare. "Wilk Kopi Luwak coffee beans. Only the best. And this piece of genius" – he tapped his coffee machine – "is a Jura E8 bean-to-cup Automatic Coffee machine. They don't make them like this just anywhere, I'll tell you that."

The coffee machine made a slight gurgle, but not an unpleasant one – less like a nasty drunk woman gurgle, more like a posh woman drinking tea type of gurgle; if there were such variations of gurgles.

"Do you take it black?" the man asked, taking two almost full cups from the coffee machine, placing them on the side and opening the fridge, where he withdrew a carton of milk.

He poured a splash in one of the cups then turned to Gray.

"Well? Black or not black?"

"Er..." For lack of a better response, he found his stunned lips responding with, "Black."

"I thought so. You look like a black man."

Gray frowned.

Was that meant to be a joke?

The man put the milk back in the fridge.

Gray looked to the back door. The path was clear. He could run. He could do it, damn he could do it.

If only he could move.

By the time he'd decided he was going to have to move, it was too late. The man was inches away from him, handing him a black cup of coffee. Gray's wide-open eyes stared at the cup. The coffee smelt magnificent.

"Cheers," the man said, then took a sip. After his sip, he

looked at the cup and said, "Damn, that's good coffee. Tim Dixon Copper cups as well, no less."

Gray nodded. A slow, subdued nod. Like he'd been concussed and was just starting to understand what was happening again.

"Would you like to sit?"

"Wh– what…" Gray managed, starting to notice the thudding of his heart, the racing thoughts bashing against the prison of his mind.

Why the hell was he having a coffee with this guy?

Why the hell was this guy giving him a coffee?

"Wh– what are you doing?" Gray finally managed to ask, briefly appreciating his own progress in finally speaking.

"What am I doing?" the man repeated, as if it was the most preposterous question ever asked of a human being. "I'm drinking some damn good coffee, that's what I'm doing. What are you doing?"

"I… er…"

The man walked over to the table and kicked a chair out.

"Sit," he instructed.

"I, er…"

"*Sit,*" he repeated, the first sign of venom in his voice.

Gray obeyed. The man then sat beside him, taking another sip on his coffee.

"Drink up. I don't want good coffee like that going to waste."

Gray lifted the cup to his mouth and, as he wondered what on earth he was doing, he took a large sip of a rich aromatic blend that tasted bloody delicious.

"Good, huh?" the man said.

Gray nodded.

"Lovely. Right, now we're sat down, and we have our coffee, would you mind terribly telling me what the fuck you are doing in my house?"

25

THIS WAS ABSOLUTE BLOODY HEAVEN, AND LUKE WAS LOVING IT.

It was like a free-for-all of useless, expensive junk. Numerous holes were appearing in the lining of his bin bag from the pointed ends of all the fancy items he'd grabbed – all of which could get them more than the thirteen thousand they needed.

He bounced to the next room – a bedroom.

Honestly, how many bedrooms does one guy need?

Did he have staff living in them? Relatives? Family?

So far, there had been no photos in any of the bedrooms. In fact, they didn't look lived in. Every bed had been made and every piece of wooden furniture was coated in a light graze of dust. Luke wondered if the guy ever actually came up here.

Such a waste.

As a child he'd had to share a bedroom with Gray. It wasn't until Gray left for university that he was actually awarded his own private bedroom, but that's only because Gray never came back to occupy the other bed.

Yet, here was this guy, with a ridiculous amount of bedrooms.

There were so many people living in poverty that could occupy those beds!

Yet, here they remained... Unoccupied and unused...

Honestly, after witnessing the interior of this ridiculously oversized egocentric mansion, he had no guilt or regret in robbing it, and no sympathy for the man who would arrive home and probably not even notice what was missing.

He had enough. His bag was bursting, and he was sure Amber had enough too.

"Amber!" he shouted out, waiting for a reply.

Nothing.

It was a big floor, she probably didn't hear him.

He made his way back to the lift, where they had said they would meet, and dumped his bag.

He waited, listening for approaching footsteps or movement or something that would indicate she was done.

How long did it take her?

"Amber!" he tried again.

Her name rebounded back to him multiple times in an empty echo.

He huffed, put his hands in his pocket, and wandered aimlessly from one wall to the other.

He imagined living here.

Imagined a different woman in every room. Endless food from his chef. The biggest and best room for his healthy mum to come visit.

His mates would be damn impressed by this abode.

He huffed. Looked to his watch. It had been almost twenty minutes. He should have arranged a time to meet.

He meandered toward the window, where he stood, looking out upon the driveway below, coated in darkness. The distant street light of the road was hidden between a far row of trees, the outline of the gates barely recognisable from this far away.

So far, no one could hear you scream...

He laughed at the thought. A silly joke, probably not that funny, but it amused him.

He huffed.

Where was that damn girl?

He leant against the window, peering out, gazing at the perfectly-groomed grass – grass that would be perfect with two sets of goal posts. He and his mates would have an awesome kickabout on a pitch like that. Maybe they could put a small changing room between the bushes and the Mercedes.

His body tensed so abruptly he stopped breathing.

The Mercedes.

He strode in the direction Amber had walked in, this time with more purpose, more haste.

"Amber!" he called out.

He marched through the first bedroom, where he found draws emptied, and through the next one.

Into a corridor lined with doors, so many doors, doors that led to God-knows-where.

And almost no light to guide his way.

"Amber?" he shouted again, this time less of a scream, more of an inquisitive wonder. "Amber, are you there?"

He put his hand on the wall to guide him forward.

He tried the first door to his right, the first door to his left, and tried the next, and the next, and the next and the next and the next.

None would open.

Why was this guy so keen to lock his doors? Who was he locking them from?

And what was he locking inside?

"Amber!" he tried again, this time with more exasperation. "Amber, come on!"

Thinking he heard something, he stopped still, silencing the shuffle of his clothes.

He listened intently.

And then he heard it.

The distant scream of his sister followed by his name.

Without another thought, he ran from door to door, calling out her name and hoping she would keep shouting back.

26

THE MAN FINISHED HIS COFFEE WITH A SATISFYING SLURP AND placed the cup down upon his smooth leather coaster.

"I– I…" Gray stuttered, searching for an answer to the question *why the fuck are you in my house* that wouldn't prompt this man to either call the police or try to detain Gray himself.

"Good Lord, spit it out," the man insisted. He was sat with his chin resting on his fist, his elbow resting on the table, and his other hand resting on the knee of his wide-open legs.

Gray could feel his body shrinking smaller and smaller.

The door. A few yards behind the man. Could he make it?

"You keep looking at that door," the man observed. "You keep staring at it, over my shoulder. What is it about that door?"

Gray didn't answer.

"Is it because you're planning to try and run for it, is that what it is? Is it?"

Gray turned his feet. Prepared his hands.

He was going to do it.

He was going to run past this guy and get out.

"Don't be a fool, my friend."

Too late.

Gray leapt to his feet and sprinted.

He didn't get more than three steps.

The man held out his arm, sturdy and flexed, his fist in a ball, and Gray ran right into it.

The man's hand then found its way to Gray's throat. Without any struggling or shaking of his bicep, he lifted Gray into the air and slammed him down upon the table.

The man's face had changed. It was no longer accommodating like he had first appeared, or questioning like he was a second ago – now it was rage. Pure, unadulterated, unleashed, flying rage. Wrath. Scorned hostility. Every one of his pores burst with the anticipation of Gray's death.

"You think..." the man spoke between heavy breaths, squeezing his hand tighter and tighter over Gray's throat, "that you... can just... come into... my house... then run past me... like that..."

Gray punched and punched against the man's arm, but, just as he'd expected, his punches were untrained and weak and feeble and had as much effect as if a toddler was fighting against him, as much effect as if he was trying to coerce a pole to move.

Gray thought nothing of fear, nothing of death – as his mind hadn't gone there yet. All he was aware of was that he could not breathe. His throat was being squeezed so tightly it was collapsing, his oesophagus so squished that no matter how much he wheezed or tried to cough or tried to suck in the relief of a clean intake of oxygen, the man was not affording him such pleasures.

In an abrupt spurt of strength, the man picked Gray up again and threw him into the depths of the kitchen.

Gray landed on his knees, sucking in breath as he ignored the pain in his kneecap.

"Hey," the man said, holding his hands out, a big, teasing

grin beaming down at Gray. "I'm only kidding! Only joking with you. What do you think I am? Some kind of psycho?"

Gray stroked his throat, feeling the indents of where the man's thumbs had just been. He was breathing, but not easily. His throat still felt squashed, still felt like his neck was collapsing inward.

"If you want to leave," the man said, "then you are welcome to try that door as much as you want."

"Please…" Gray managed, finally finding the guts to beg. "We didn't mean to…"

"Didn't mean to what? Break into my home? Invade my sanctuary? Rob me?"

"We didn't, it's our mum, she's sick…"

The man's grin extended even further. "Did you just say – *we?*"

"Wh– what?"

"You mean, there's more of you?"

Gray bowed his head.

He'd just set his brother and sister up to this sadistic arsehole.

"Please, we don't mean you any harm," Gray repeated.

"Tell me your name."

"Please, just–"

"I am not going to ask you again. What – is – your – name?"

"… Graham."

"Graham? You don't look like a Graham."

"My friends call me Gray."

"Gray? What, like the fifty shades guy? You like him, is that why they call you that? You all into dominating and lycra and sex games, is that it?"

"No… It's just a shortened version of my name…"

The man nodded, confirming that he would accept this answer. He took a step toward Gray, who remained crouched, and took something out of his pocket – something that looked like a button or a remote control or something like that.

Gray backed away, expecting a weapon, and was honestly relieved.

"Hey, Gray?" the man said.

"What?" Gray weakly replied.

"Want to see something cool?"

Gray shook his head. At least, he thought he did, but his head barely moved.

The man pressed the button.

A sudden chug began, some kind of electric motor, a heavy movement. Metal shook and the moon began to disappear.

Gray looked to the windows. To the door.

Outside of them, metal shutters descended, going lower and lower and lower.

Gray had no choice but to try to get out. He ran past the man and the man let him.

By the time he had opened the back door the shutters were all the way down, blocking his escape.

He charged against the shutters, but they didn't even buckle. They were solid, as good as brick, impenetrable.

Gray looked back at the man.

"What are you doing?" Gray asked.

The man replied with a grin, nothing else.

"What kind of place is this?"

The man dropped the remote to the floor.

"Please, let us out."

The man lifted his foot.

"Please…"

The man stomped his foot downwards, landing his heel on the remote. He lifted his foot again, landing his heel once more, then once more, then once more – until, eventually, the remote was nothing but empty casing and a wiry mess.

"Looks like you're trapped in here with me, Gray."

Gray would like to say he was thinking of his sister, or his brother, or even his mum, at this point.

But he wasn't.

All he was thinking of was this strange man before him, who the hell this guy really was, and how much longer he had left of his life.

27

LUKE WAS BOXED IN BY DARKNESS. HE RAN TO THE WINDOWS, HIS mind grappling with a muddle of thoughts that were unsuccessfully attempting to make sense of the situation.

Metal shutters descended with a sinister rattling, a slow omen of isolation.

He pulled on the base of the windows with all he had, but they responded with a strength he couldn't fight.

He rushed into a nearby room, knocking the door open with his shoulder, only to see three windows also being covered by shutters.

He returned to the window of the corridor and punched it with his fist, attempting to smash it, but barely making it shake.

He whirred his fist up, pulled it back, imagined the face of his father in the reflection and poured his fist forward with all he had.

This time, it shook.

He did the same again, pouring his anger into the lunge of his fist. One thing Luke knew was how to throw a punch, and how to take the pain to his knuckles.

When the glass did eventually smash, Luke clutched his fist

and brushed the minute shards of glass from his fingers – fingers that were now glistening with small specks of blood.

The pain could wait.

The blood could wait.

Ignoring it, he placed his fists upon the shutter. He rattled and rattled it, only to find it was too sturdy to be rattled.

He punched the shutters and winced. This wasn't glass – this was metal. Thick, impenetrable metal.

And, without having to see any more windows, he knew they were shut in.

"Luke!" came the scream of Amber's voice, his own name barely distinguishable in the screech of her panic.

"Amber! Amber, where are you?"

Luke dashed from door to door, opening each.

He turned a corridor, stumbling as his sprinting legs skidded, and finally found his sister.

She was on the far side of this corridor, on her knees, crying and shrieking in front of an open door.

"Amber!" Luke cried, running toward her. "Amber, what is it?"

Luke slid to his knees, halting next to her and pulling her close. His arms tightened, his hand gently pushing her head into the dip of his shoulder.

"Amber, are you okay?"

He knew it was a stupid question as soon as he asked.

She was evidently not okay.

But, amongst her weeping and fretting and huffs of hysteria he could not make out why she was so frenzied.

She couldn't have seen the shutters yet.

Was it guilt?

Was she finding it so difficult to fight between saving their mum and doing something immoral?

"It's okay, it's okay," Luke told her. "We are doing this for

Mum, just remember that. It's our only choice. This guy doesn't need everything he has."

"No…" Amber managed, making a visible effort to calm her crying. "No…"

"What do you mean, no?"

"That's not it…"

"Then what's the matter?"

She pulled her head from his reassurance and looked at him, red bags forming beneath her eyes.

"We have to leave," she said, suddenly so coherently and so confidently. "We have to leave – *now.*"

"Fine, we have what we need, we can go."

"No, Luke, you don't understand."

"What don't I understand? What is it?"

Amber lifted a drooping finger and directed it toward the door behind her.

"Is he in there?" Luke asked, jumping to his only logical explanation.

"No… No…"

Luke took his arms from around Amber, slowly letting her go, and pushed himself to his feet.

"What is it then?" Luke inquired.

"Don't go in there… Don't look…"

Of course he was going to look.

He crept forward, stepping into the room, his hand searching the wall for a light switch. He had to take a few more steps in until he found one.

The ugly glow of an artificial light brightened the room.

Luke's eyes were immediately drawn to a sight that he knew he would be seeing in nightmares for years to come.

He backed away.

Turned off the light.

Shut the door.

Looked to Amber, wanting to start weeping and fretting with her.

"Holy shit…" he gasped.

Robbing this place didn't matter anymore.

They could rob somewhere else.

They were shuttered in.

There were bodies in the room.

Then Amber muttered the only words that could make it worse:

"The car… He's here… He's inside…"

THE MAN CROUCHED BEFORE GRAY, LIKE YOU WOULD WHEN about to pet a cat or ask a child about the knee they'd just wounded.

"How many of you are there, Gray?" the man asked.

Gray's lips stuttered over syllables that dropped to the tiled kitchen floor without any coherence.

He didn't want to give away Amber and Luke's presence.

At the same time, he really didn't want to die.

"I'll ask you again – who are you here with, Gray?"

"N– n– nobody... I'm alone..."

Despite overflowing with terror, he felt a little pride in the bravery he'd just shown by lying.

Unfortunately, it didn't look like the guy bought it. The man nodded, briefly closing his eyes, as if to say, *so that's how we're going to play it?*

The man stood. Gray tried to use the opportunity to run, but the man simply thwacked the sole of his Salvatore Ferragamo Moccasin size twelves into Gray's face, effortlessly repeating this action until Gray's head dizzied upon the impact of the hard kitchen floor.

The man took a pair of pliers from a drawer.

Gray thought it was an odd thing to keep in a kitchen drawer – but, from the look of the other utensils in the drawer, it didn't look like where the man kept his cutlery.

The man knelt before Gray again.

"Give me your hand," he instructed, ever so calmly, ever so confident.

So confident, in fact, that Gray was tempted to obey – but he didn't. He didn't move his hand out the way either – it was as if, by keeping his hand exactly where it was, he was neither demonstrating refusal nor defiance.

"I said, give me your hand," the man instructed again.

"N– no…" Gray whimpered.

The man's hand had clamped around Gray's wrist before Gray could realise what was happening. He was starting to feel more and more dizzy, and he wasn't sure if it was from concussion or a constant state of anxiety.

The man clamped his arm over Gray's elbow, causing Gray to twist into a position where a slight bit of pressure on the elbow would cause him an exceedingly large amount of pain.

The man held Gray's fingers firmly and locked his pliers onto Gray's thumbnail.

"Who else is here, Gray?" the man repeated.

Gray did not know what to do. Should he object to the pain? Give away his siblings? Be brave and keep claiming he was alone?

His thought process took too long and the man didn't hesitate. The pliers clamped around Gray's thumb nail and the man pulled with a violent yank. It took a few more yanks – three to be precise – but, after shifting the nail a little further each time, the bizarre sight of a nail-less thumb appeared amongst a pool of gushing red.

Gray saw his own nail thud to the ground, almost hidden in

a pool of blood that fell like water from a gutter. He screamed and he wept and he protested, though he did not threaten – instead, he begged for it to end. He could feel the thick, warm moisture of blood sticking his fingers together, and the violence of it was provoking his gag reflex.

"I'm going to ask you again," the man said, as Gray felt the pliers clamp over the nail currently attached to his forefinger. "Who else are you in here with?"

Gray considered his options again.

But, just as he felt pressure to his nail and a slight pull was applied, he spilt the beans like a clumsy chef.

"Okay, okay! There are two more!" he cried out, hating himself – but his desire to escape torment outweighed his self-hatred.

"Tell me about them."

"Er, erm," Gray frantically attempted to think of what useful information he could give. "A girl, a boy…"

"How do you know them?"

"They are my brother and sister."

"And what are their names?"

"Amber and Luke."

"And where are they?"

"They– they– they started on the top floor!"

The man let go of Gray's arm and stood, placing the pliers on the side with an arrogant thud.

Gray took his thumb in his hand and stared at the stump of gooey red skin where his nail used to be. He wasn't sure what was more agonising – the pain, or the sight of his thumb without a nail.

"Thank you, Gray. You have been most kind."

"Please, please don't hurt them."

The man said nothing. He just smiled a sneaky, slanted smile.

"We only did this to save our mum."

"Your mum?"

"She has months left to live, and the only chance we had was to put her in a drug trial that costs thirteen thousand pound, and we don't have anywhere near that much."

"Is that so?"

"Yes, and that's why we are here, I swear, that's why."

The man nodded, his face twisting to a thoughtful contortion, as if this was interesting news, and he could do something with it.

From the man's reaction, Gray wasn't sure whether revealing this was a great idea or not. He was hoping for sympathy, but he was beginning to learn that this man had little of it.

"Are you just doing this because we broke in?"

The man sighed.

He opened a cupboard and withdrew an apron. It was white, stained in ketchup, with *let me feed you strawberries* written on it in Comic Sans.

"Wh– what are you doing?"

"I'm putting an apron on, Gray," the man said, placing the apron over his head.

"Why?"

"Because I don't want to get any mess on my suit."

The man finished tying the apron behind his back. He stood over Gray, sighing, his hands on his hips, going from decision to decision.

"So," the man declared. "How should I do it, Gray?"

"What? Do what?"

"I like to do it slow, but I tell you what, seeing as there's a girl upstairs, I think I'd rather do it slow with her."

"What? Do what slow?"

"Amber would be, of course, far more to my taste. I don't

find killing men as satisfying." He clapped his hands together to signal a decisive moment. "That's it! I have decided."

"What? Decided what?"

"I am going to do it quick, Gray. Nice and clean and quick." He crouched down, grinning a grin that sent a waterfall of dread pouring down his skin. "That way, I will have more time for your sister."

29

ONCE AMBER'S THOUGHTS HAD MORPHED FROM NONSENSICAL leaps of panics to thoughts that could bear some coherence, she grew quickly aware that Gray was still downstairs on his own.

And that he hadn't chimed the grandfather clock.

Which either meant that he hadn't noticed the car outside, or he had been unable to chime it.

Maybe he'd run away. Maybe he'd left them there. Maybe he was halfway down the drive right at that very moment.

Or maybe he'd been discovered, and...

And what?

Luke emerged from the room where she'd found the morbidly decorated corpses with his face just as pale as hers.

He paused for a moment, leaning against the wall.

She could almost see his thoughts jumping from drastic decision to drastic decision. He'd been quicker to adjust to the sight than she had, and she was sure that he was now trying to decide what their next move was.

"We... we have to get out of here," he mumbled. "We need to get out of here quickly."

"Luke–"

"The windows aren't an option. Some kind of shutters... I... I don't know how..."

She tried to decipher the code.

Windows? Shutters?

"What are you talking about?" she asked, finding herself speaking louder than she intended.

In an unexpected spurt of energy Luke grabbed her hand, pulled her from the floor, and dragged her through the corridor until they reached a window.

His hand raised to indicate the shutters that had them trapped in.

She ran from that window to the next, around the corner to the smashed window where she could press her open palms against the shutters, feeling their resilience to her meek force.

"How – how is he doing this?" she asked.

"I have no idea."

"What do we do?" She turned to look, hopping from one foot to the other, her fingers interlocking and wrapping around each other like a tub of frantic snakes.

"We have to hope it's not on every floor."

They checked the next floor down. Rushing to every window and finding just what they expected to find.

Amber stopped in the corner of a corridor and she collapsed, curling into a ball, huddling her arms around her knees, rocking back and forth and shaking her head, refusing, refusing to think.

What about Mum?

How would Mum get the treatment if they never got out?

Luke didn't force her to stand up, didn't pull her away or tell her to get a grip. Instead, he sat next to her, tucked his arms around her and held her in a silent embrace for the next few minutes.

"It's okay," Luke eventually said. "We'll get out, it's okay."

"What about Mum?"

"We'll… we'll find a way. Let's just get out, then we'll find a way."

"Luke, what about – what about Gray?"

The look on Luke's face provided the evidence Amber needed to confirm Luke hadn't been thinking about Gray.

"I think we may just have to concentrate on us," Luke decided. "For now."

"I'm not leaving him."

"Amber, you saw the bodies. Didn't you?"

She pushed her lips together as she held back tears. She nodded.

"I don't want to leave him. Honestly. But he's on the bottom floor – chances are, if he could get out, he already would have."

"And if he couldn't have?"

Luke didn't answer.

He stood.

"We can't just wait around here," he said. "We need to find a way out."

Amber looked around. The corridor was soaked with darkness, no late evening light seeping in through any window.

"Come on," he prompted.

Amber didn't move, so he took her arm and forced her to her feet.

"Let's get to the ground floor, as slowly as we can," he said.

"The ground floor?"

"Surely it would be the best place to find a way out?"

He guided her to the stairs, and down another floor, where she halted.

"But – what if he's there?"

Luke went to answer, but somehow his answer was interrupted by the manic screams of their brother coming from below.

30

THE MAN HAD EXPECTED GRAY TO RUN.

One thing he had found from experience was that human behaviour was highly predictable.

Not that it's silly to try and run from immediate danger, of course not – it's instinct. It's just that they all ran the same way with the same expression and the same terror smacked across their face.

It was just too easy for the man to hastily withdraw a sharp kitchen knife, dive to his knees, and stick it into the back of a fleeing heel of the predictable oaf trying to escape.

Escape.

Hah!

Where did he expect to escape to?

They were shuttered in.

Again, the predictability. People will run even if there is nowhere to run to. They will hide until they are found, and him finding them was as inevitable as death or birth or anything in between.

Gray screamed as he collapsed.

The man admired his work, the blade sticking out at a perfect point from the rear of Gray's foot.

Gray screamed again as the man snatched the knife out.

He let Gray drag himself out of the room, leaving a bloody trail that was going to be a bitch to clean up later.

But he wanted Gray to reach the base of the stairs, as it meant the other two would be able to see their brother's corpse from above. He wanted to scare them, to draw them out, to push them to revealing their position or, at the very least, become reckless with fear.

So he trailed slowly behind, watching Gray slime forward. Like a snail, leaving a line of gunk behind him.

He made himself laugh at the simile.

Luckily, the floor wasn't carpet. Otherwise he would not be laughing.

Finally, Gray reached the base of the stairs.

This is where he wanted to do it.

He strode forward this time, walking with a purpose he previously hadn't, and plunged the knife into the back of Gray's right thigh.

Another scream.

Predictable.

Why do they always scream? Especially when shuttered inside a house at least three-hundred yards from any other.

What do they hope to accomplish?

He plunged the knife into the base of Gray's spine.

Gray's entire nervous system responded. Flinching, spasming, his right arm shooting out, his legs flickering with random energy.

After the flickers had died down, Gray tried to use his body, but found himself unable.

The man enjoyed this part the most. When he could see their hope fading. When paralysis would set in and they couldn't move yet they still tried, still adamantly struggling against it, still somehow believing they were going to suddenly be able to use their limbs again.

Gray wasn't going to move or walk any time soon.

Or ever again, for that matter.

A gentle thundering of footsteps came from above.

They had heard. They were about to witness it.

Gray didn't want to deny them the show.

He tightened his apron, ensuring he was not about to ruin his suit.

He went to his knee beside Gray's head, grabbed the back of his victim's hair and lifted the hopeless face.

Gray's eyes still darted back and forth, still denying what was about to happen, still rejecting what was inevitable.

The man, wanting to show off what he was doing, looked up.

There they were.

The girl – Amber.

The boy – Luke.

Both peering over a banister, staring down, looking for the source of the sound of their brother's pain.

And, for the two seconds in which their eyes met, his dick hardened and his body tingled. He held their eyes for those two long seconds, dragging them out into slow motion, searching their souls as they searched his.

They wouldn't find one.

He swung the knife and stuck it into the exposed skin of Gray's throat, just half an inch beside his Adam's apple, and twisted it.

The two faces disappeared with a gasp, and their feet thudded the soundtrack to their departure.

Gray's mouth hung open, sucking in air that never arrived, a trickle of outward breath without any breath in it.

He withdrew the knife and stuck it into Gray's throat again. This time he dragged it across, cutting Gray's Adam's apple in two, slicing it like afternoon fruit, taking the knife back out again once a complete one-hundred-and-eighty-degree slit had been formed.

He let go of Gray's hair, letting the head thump to the surface.

Gray's body was empty. The population of thoughts had escaped the home of his mind. The fear had been removed.

It was foreplay.

Damn good foreplay, but that was all it was.

But, as we all know, as is predictably inevitable, foreplay has to end and the real pleasure has to begin.

He began to climb the stairs.

HE WAS DEAD.

Gray was dead.

Was he dead?

She'd seen a knife enter his throat, but she'd moved away before she could see his dead face.

Oh, God.

Did I just think those words?

Dead... face...

His dead face.

He could still be alive.

Couldn't he?

She shook her head and covered her face with her hands.

Even if she didn't acknowledge it to herself, she knew that it was denial. The most common yet useless of human reactions.

The guy had stuck a knife into Gray's throat and twisted it.

There was no ambulance coming.

No help was on the way.

There was no way he could survive that...

"He's dead..." she whispered, not sure why she suddenly had to say it aloud.

"Come on!" Luke urged her, grabbing her arm, but it was like grabbing hold of a tree or someone walking in water.

The next image that projected into the slideshow of horrors in her mind was that of the man. Unblemished skin, smoothed down collar, top button done up, apron over suit, hair gelled to the side, swept with precision – this *man*.

The guy driving the Mercedes.

Killing Gray.

Killing.

Gray.

Killing.

"Amber! Move!"

She looked to his arm, still attached to hers, hurting from the grip around her bicep but feeling none of the pain.

"I have to see…" she said.

"What? Have to see what?"

"If he's dead… I have to see…"

She edged back to the banister, but Luke pulled her away.

"We have to hide! Get out of here! Call the police or something!"

"We don't have our phones…"

"We don't have time!"

"I have to… I have to see…"

She edged back to the banister. He held onto her.

"Amber, please," he said, no longer confident or forceful, but weak and pleading.

"I have to…"

He reluctantly let her go, standing back, and she peered over the banister once more.

Sure enough, Gray's motionless body lay face down in an ever-expanding pool of blood. Her hands covered her gasp but there was little else she could do.

Gray had just been murdered before her.

Murdered before her.

Murdered.

The man looked up.

She saw him, but she didn't.

Of course, she looked at him, watching as he walked up the stairs, looking back up at her – but she didn't consciously acknowledge him, same as she hadn't acknowledged the colour of the floorboards or creak of the steps, such was her focus on Gray.

The man caught her eye. He was on the second floor now, approaching the third.

He was walking slowly. Why wasn't he running? Why was he just grinning at them, instead of chasing them?

Because he knows we're trapped... That we have nowhere we can run...

He entered the stairs of the third floor, still looking up, still beaming that lecherous smirk.

"Amber!"

Luke's screaming of her name snapped her out of a trance she hadn't consented to.

This time she allowed him to pull her away, allowed his hand to clasp tightly around her arm and drag her down the corridor.

"You're hurting me," she said, but her voice was lost.

Luke tried the next door, and the next, and the next, meeting nothing but locked doors.

They could hear his footsteps now.

They could hear him approaching.

Luke barged into a door, wishing it would buckle, but nothing. Absolutely nothing.

They turned a corner, moving from a brisk walk to a run. Luke could now let go of Amber's arm, assured that she would follow, and was able to use both hands to try opening doors.

He finally found one that was open.

They entered it and immediately regretted doing so.

THIS HAD WORKED OUT PERFECTLY.

As far as he was concerned, anyway.

There they were on the fifth floor, trying doors and seeing if one was unlocked. They would be rushing from locked door to locked door, maybe even trying to bash one down, maybe even barge one open.

But there was only one room that was unlocked.

And he knew which one it was.

And he hoped they found it.

He grinned, picturing their reaction as they entered.

The trophy room.

His favourite room.

In the middle of the room, a swivel chair, which could turn to any of the walls. On every wall, four lines of shelves, perfect distance from one another, the top and bottom equal distance from the ceiling and floor respectively.

On them, his trophies.

In boxes and cabinets with transparent screens that would allow him to sit there in an evening and admire his skillset.

Everyone has a talent.

And at school, they were encouraged to explore their talents.

At his school, which was the best of the best, everyone had many talents. Violin, piano, rugby, art, drama, whatever – but no one had a talent like he did.

And that first trophy was from the school bully, on the far bottom left of the left wall.

Just a single finger, kept in cool conditions to preserve it perfectly. The middle finger too, metaphorically removing the bully's ability to say *fuck you* to anyone else.

Before he fed Eve and Sheila to his pigs, he planned to pick his trophy and display it proudly along with the others.

Eve was a whore, so she needed something that fit her role. He could take her tongue, maybe, which he had found to be her strongest asset, and place it next to the carved clitoris of the German exchange student he'd met in Glasgow three years ago.

Sheila was an innocent little child and he had treasured her smile, but he had enough lips already. He could also say she had a good heart, but he had three of them.

He liked her hair. Maybe a few strands would do.

Gray.

Ooh, Gray.

He wasn't a particularly good-looking fellow. He wasn't necessarily bad looking, but there were no features that stuck out as *must-haves*.

He wondered what Luke and Amber would be like.

Ooh, Amber. From the brief glance he'd been afforded, he had deduced that she was pretty.

There were many parts of her he'd like to keep.

He reached the fifth floor.

He looked down at his apron as he sauntered through the corridor. It was a mess, and he wanted to be presentable when he finally met Amber and Luke.

You only have one chance to make a first impression.

He took it off.

He didn't want to mess up his suit, but he had plenty, he could afford to lose it. And he wouldn't be willing to do that with just anyone! There weren't many bodies he'd be happy to throw out a suit for.

But he could already taste Amber, and she tasted so good.

Like a child's vitamins.

As adults, vitamins were just a solid tablet, had little to excite you. But, when he was a child, his mother would give him squishy vitamins, strawberry or orange or lemon ones, with the texture of jelly babies.

He would squish the vitamin between his teeth and let the juices burst out.

Oh, Amber.

I can't wait.

He turned the corridor, smiling at the sight of the open door to his trophy room.

They better not have touched anything.

33

THE SIGHT DIDN'T QUITE REGISTER IN AMBER'S MIND.

It was as if it was too much. As if the obscure violence and abstract images were just too extreme to be conceived. As if her mind was already full enough, like an overflowing bucket of water, and adding another horrific sight just meant that it hit the water and fell down the sides.

Luke's grip on Amber's hand, his open-mouthed stare that circled around the wall, and his weak muttering of, "Oh, dear God," prompted Amber to perhaps realise that something was immensely off.

Slowly, it began to seep in.

A hand here. A heart there. A finger, a rake of skin, a deformed slice of tongue.

Some of it she couldn't even make out. Couldn't even deduce what body part it was. It was so disgustingly original, so vividly unique, that, by itself, it was barely recognisable from what it had been attached to.

The thoughts slowly crept into her consciousness.

These are body parts.

These came from people.

There are a lot of them.

There are a lot of body parts.

There are a lot of body parts that came from people.

Without still fully understanding how or why or when or who or what, Amber's produced a high-pitched piercing scream.

Luke's hand clasped over her mouth, halting the sound, but she didn't feel it, nor could she tell that he was behind her or whispering to listen very, very carefully to a set of steps that were coming closer.

Amber finally looked away from the items to see Luke peering out of the doorway.

Steps.

Steps of someone.

Steps of the man who...

Luke slammed the door shut and twisted the lock. He took a few paces back and listened to the steps as they ended, stopping firmly and precisely outside that door.

The door handle slowly rotated, but the door wouldn't open, and the handle returned to its original position.

Luke stared at the door handle, watching its movement cease, watching as it remained still, watching as it did not rotate again.

Amber was still only partly aware of this, still digesting the mass of items.

She wondered which item of hers was going to end up here.

And, just as she realised she was wondering it, she realised that she had almost resigned herself to death.

And she shouldn't.

That's when she came around. When she turned to Luke, then turned to look at the door he was staring at.

"What is it?" she asked.

Luke said nothing. Just kept his eyes peeled wide and pointed absently at the door.

"Who is there?" Amber shouted.

"Shut up!" Luke snapped.

Amber, for some reason, didn't shut up. She didn't know why she was trying to speak to the man, didn't know why she was engaging him, but she somehow felt safe to do so. As if she could remember Luke turning the lock at some point, and so knew that he wasn't coming in any time soon.

"What do you want?" she shouted again.

"What the fuck are you doing?" Luke said in a hushed shout.

Amber ignored him.

"Just let us go."

No movement. No turn of the door handle. The man didn't speak.

That is, until he did.

"Let me in, Amber," the man's voice, confident and smooth, spoke.

She looked to Luke, both of them sharing the same thought.

How does he know my name?

"Tell Luke to open the door."

They looked to each other again, wide eyes, terrified wonder.

Then Luke bowed his head as he realised.

"Gray," Luke said. "He sold us out. He told him."

Gray is dead.

The thought hit Amber unexpectedly. As if it was the only thing she could associate with Gray.

Dead.

Ceased to exist.

Murdered.

Not the memories of growing up, of the kind face, of the arguments – just that he was dead.

Like when you go through a break-up and hear a song, then all you can ever think of when you hear that song is that break-up.

All that his name conjured was *death*.

"I'm not going away," the man said.

"Well we ain't letting you in!" Luke shouted.

"You think I don't have a key?" the man said, followed by laughter. "This is *my* house. You think I don't have a key to every room?"

Luke went to shout back but his syllables didn't form.

He looked around. They both did. Trying to ignore the trophies, trying to find another way.

But the room was like a box. There was one way in and out. The rest of the walls were adorned with...

He did this.

As if she hadn't thought it already, she thought it now.

He made these.

How many people did it take to create this quantity of trophies?

The man's steps began and grew fainter.

Luke let go of a breath he didn't know he was holding.

"What do we do?" he asked Amber.

Amber looked back at him peculiarly.

What do they do?

So far she had been completely reliant on Luke, reliant on his snapping her out of her trances, taking her away from danger, finding her when she was screaming.

Now he was asking her?

How the hell was she supposed to know?

The footsteps returned, growing louder and stopping outside the door.

The sound of a key entering a keyhole and turning was the only thing louder than their thudding heartbeats.

The locks twisted and turned and the room was unlocked.

Luke went to move, as if to force the door shut – but by the time the thought had occurred to him, the door handle had already twisted, the door had opened, and the man was standing there looking directly at them.

HE HATED CLICHÉS AND DUMB EXPRESSIONS – JUST LIKE HE hated the predictability of people's reactions to immediate death.

But, on this occasion, there was one idiom that just summed up the sight before him too succinctly:

Like a deer caught in the headlights.

And that was precisely what they were.

Two deers, caught in the headlights – and surrounded by everyone else who had ever been scared by him, no less.

"Please," the girl, Amber, said. "Please don't hurt us."

Again, predictability.

Infuriating.

Please don't hurt us.

Please let me go.

Please don't kill me.

No one that had ever said that to him had been successful in their request – and people had said it to him many, many times. To him, it was practically the same as saying *cheese sandwich,* or *would you like coleslaw?*

Did these people really think he was ever going to acquiesce their request?

Honestly, the best thing that one could say in this moment was something to throw him off.

Once, when one of his subordinates had become irritable in his presence, he had simply looked at the ranting idiot and said: "My walls aren't four foot high."

The inferior employee had gone to speak, stopped, twisted his face and said "…eh?"

Because it was unexpected. It threw him.

Honestly, instead of begging, say something original, then at least it brings some amusement to their predicament.

"Please," Amber pleaded again.

He stepped forward.

The boy, Luke, put his arm across Amber and tucked him behind her.

"Don't fucking touch us," Luke said.

Now this made him smile.

Don't fucking touch us.

Genius. So hostile, so angry. And the boy said it with utter venom, like Luke hated him so much that there was nothing Luke could do to contain it.

He admired it.

"Come any closer and I'll break your fucking fingers," Luke said.

The man couldn't help it. His mouth opened and guffawed a giant "Hah!" in Luke's direction.

He withdrew the knife still dripping with their brother's blood and held it by his waist, loosely but definitely, just so they could see it.

"What is your fucking problem?" Luke asked, shouting now, getting louder.

The man looked around the room, admiring his work. Smiling broadly at what he'd done. Knowing that this would tell them how much he was looking forward to choosing which part of them would be trophesised.

Trophesised, he thought. *I think I've just invented a word. And a jolly good word too...*

This glance around the room at his art, however, was his first and only mistake. As, in the gleam of his eyes or the raising of his smile, he had given away just how proud he was, just how pleased he was with all the items in this room. How much he treasured them.

Because Luke seemed to notice this too.

Luke leapt to the nearest box, displaying the finger of a mixed-race woman with the nail still painted red, and shoved the box to the floor, its glass screen smashing into broken shards.

"No!" the man cried out.

Luke rushed to another and put his hand behind it.

The man rushed forward and, noticing that Luke hadn't pushed this box off but was instead holding his hand in readiness to do so, he halted.

Watched Luke. Waited for the next move.

"Yeah, that's it," said Luke, a gloating sneer to his voice. "You don't want me to wreck any more of these, do you?"

The man did not reply. His ever-present grin had morphed to wrath. His fingers were flexing over the knife. His decision-making skills were being tested.

"Let my sister go," Luke demanded.

"What?" Amber said, quickly turning to Luke. "What about you?"

Luke scoffed. "Look at this guy. This private school rich dick. Think I can't take him?"

"Luke..."

"Honestly, I've taken pieces of piss like this down for nothing. You get out and I'll follow."

"But Luke..."

"I'm not asking, Amber."

Luke pushed the box an inch forward, causing the man to throb.

"Let. Her. Go."

With a big intake of breath, the man nodded.

"Fine," he grumbled.

There was nowhere the girl could go anyway.

By the time she would realise that, he'd be done with Luke and be on his way to her.

Amber turned back once more and took hold of Luke's spare hand.

"Go," he instructed her.

"But–"

"I promise you. I can take him. Just go."

"I–"

"Get the police. Get help. Then come back. Honestly, I'll be fine."

With a hesitation she wiped a tear, nodded, and turned. As she crossed the man, she pushed herself against the far side of the door frame, keeping him as far away from herself as she could.

She turned the corridor and sprinted out of sight.

Luke locked eyes with the man, who returned the glare.

"Looks like it's just you and me," Luke stated.

AMBER RAN.

She had no idea where to, what for, or where her legs were going to direct her. She barged against a corridor and skidded around a corner and somehow found her way to the stairs.

She glanced over her shoulders at the shutters blocking the moonlight from the window, how had he done that, it was covering every window, every window every window every damn window trapped, trapped, trapped inside and Luke's fighting him and Gray and Gray and oh god oh god oh–

Get a grip.

She had to find a phone.

Concentrate on the task.

A phone. A phone. A phone.

Those boxes were full of body parts.

Where would a phone be?

People rarely had landlines anymore. But, surely, there must be something...

She ran down the stairs, leaping a few steps at a time until she had descended to the ground floor.

She'd forgotten that Gray's empty body was laid at the

bottom of the stairs. The expected surprise took her feet from beneath her, and she collapsed down the final few steps to the bottom floor, landing in a pool of red.

She lifted her hands up, looking at her brother's blood as if she had no idea what it was.

She nudged him, even weakly saying, "Gray? Gray, are you there?"

She didn't know why.

But she kept trying.

"Gray? Come on, wake up."

She closed her eyes. Flinched away.

This wasn't a grumpy older brother refusing to wake up for school in the morning. This was something else. This was...

Don't say it.

She was going to have to forget. As nasty as it was, she was going to have to forget that he was... that he was... that he was de...

She could grieve later.

She leapt over the body like it was an obstacle on a computer game and ran from room to room. Dodging expensive furniture, side-stepping glass tables, scanning the walls displaying such beautiful works of art.

Ignoring further stains of red in the kitchen, she eventually found it. On the wall. Black with a grey face, and a wire connecting it to the wall. She remembered having a phone like this in the house when she was eight.

She lifted it and placed it next to her ear.

She heard the glorious jarring echo of a dial tone.

Her eyes closed as she breathed out a long breath of relief. Anxiety sunk out of her like water filtered through sand, pouring into an ocean of hope.

She shoved her thumb on *9*, hitting a few other buttons at the same time. She reset the dial tone and tried again, this time taking more care in dialling *9 9 9*.

She put the phone to her ear and let it ring.

And ring.

And ring.

Why was it ringing so much?

Then came her answer.

"We are sorry, but the outgoing call function has been disabled at this time."

What?

How?

No...

Did that mean she couldn't make any calls at all?

She tried to think of her mum's landline. She wouldn't answer, it was pointless. She could, however, remember the number of the nurse who used to look after her mum, back when she first became ill and could afford such a thing.

Amber dialled the number and put the phone to her ear, letting it ring.

And ring.

And ring.

"We are sorry, but the outgoing call function has been–"

"No!" she wailed, dropping the phone, her body contorting, a folded piece of cardboard, her mind a presentation of images, each one representing another form of agony.

She tried the back door. The way they had come in.

She swung the door open and her hope lifted again, for the brief second before she saw the shutters.

She grabbed hold of the shutters and she shook and shook, and shook, and shook.

It made a huge clatter, a repeating barricade of noise, but to no avail.

"Help!" she screamed against the shutter. "Help! Please, somebody!"

But she knew it was no use.

They had gone to this house because it was so far away

from any other house. Because there was no way they would be noticed. Because neighbours wouldn't have any idea what they were doing.

And now they were trapped. Too far away from other life, in the home of a murderer.

She fell to her knees and covered her head with her arms, hoping that if she just pretended this wasn't happening, then maybe – just maybe – it wasn't.

THE STUPID BOY'S HAND WAS RESTING FIRMLY AGAINST THE BACK of a box containing five toe nails, all taken off the right foot of a ginger woman from Manchester.

This woman had been strikingly beautiful – not in the cliched sense, but in the real sense. He had always had a real distaste of artificial beauty, finding too much make-up and fake implants repulsive. He would much rather a natural face, with blemishes upon the skin and scars that showed a life lived. This woman had freckles over her nose and a long, grey, faded line beneath her chin – something from a struggle long ago. She hadn't been the kind of woman who had starved herself; he'd enjoyed her size twelve figure, her clothes encasing her body like an unwrapped gift, pressing against the ribbons, waiting to be untied.

Those five nails were the last thing that remained of her beauty. The box had been plugged into the wall, allowing a small compressor to constrict the box's vapour, raising its pressure, cooling down the gasses of the air, and absorbing any heat it may have come in contact with.

This had made the box good enough to preserve the nails for five years and eight months.

And now this boy, this imbecile named Luke, was going to wreck it.

"Let go of that box," he instructed. "Let go of it and step away."

"Why the fuck would I?" Luke retorted, prompting a sneer at the impudence. "You drop the knife, then we'll talk about me letting these body parts go, you psycho freak."

An interesting proposition.

Drop the knife and leave himself unarmed – leaving the boy with the only leverage.

Or, lunge at the boy, and hope that he could catch the box before it smashed upon the ground and the toenails were lost forever.

Hmm.

What a conundrum.

It was like he was on a gameshow. Like a presenter was giving him two options, and he had to weigh up the better one.

Option one – risk losing the nails and stab the boy.

Option two – win a million dollars.

Of course, option two was not to win a million dollars. For starters, the currency of England was pounds, and he already had a good few million of those.

He realised he'd been lost in thought and brought himself back to the room.

"Let go of the box," he instructed, taking a step forward.

"Eh!" Luke exclaimed. "Stay where you are. An' I really think me letting go is not what you want right now."

The imbecile was right. It had been a poor choice of words.

"Fine. Stop touching it."

"Like I said, the knife."

There was no chance he was losing the knife.

He began to come to terms with it. Losing the toenails.

It was his own stupid fault for leaving this room unlocked.

He *never* left this room unlocked.

He was only popping out for half an hour, he didn't think he'd have to deal with this mess when he came back.

He decided to try a different tact.

"I'm going to fuck your sister," he stated, as matter-of-factly as if he was reciting a recipe for slow-cooked veil.

"Shut up."

He took a small step forward. So small Luke's anger didn't allow Luke to notice.

"I'm going to fuck her, and I'm going to do it over your naked corpse."

"I said shut up!"

Luke was shouting now.

This was good.

Make them lose control. Make them lose it all and they relinquish any power they had.

"What's the matter? Would you rather stay alive so you can watch?"

"You touch my sister, I'll kill you."

He couldn't help but laugh – a loud, blurt of a laugh, a mocking one, one that was sure to incense this boy's feeble disposition.

"I swear, if you–"

More empty threats.

This was his chance.

He dove forward, swinging for Luke.

Luke leapt back, dodging the knife, letting go of the box. He caught it just in time, and replaced it on the shelf, leaving the way open to pace toward Luke.

Luke did what was most predictable – which, as mentioned, was a real bane of this man's life – and tried to throw his arms into the nearby trophies so he could scatter and destroy as many as he could and therefore distract the man.

The man had plunged his knife into Luke's side before he managed.

Unexpectantly, however, Luke's instinct was not to scream. This was not, as you say, his 'first rodeo.' A blade was not intimidating to him. Instead, he swung his fist up and sent it into the man's chin.

The man stumbled back.

Now he was the one annoyed.

No one had ever dared before.

What did this child think–

Foolish, to keep thinking angry thoughts, leaving his chin open for another under-hook. Before he knew it, the man had been forced out into the corridor, and the knife was no longer in his hand.

Luke was running at him with the knife above his head.

The man ducked the blade, grabbed Luke's wrist, and smacked it into the wall.

The knife went flying across the corridor, skidding along the perfectly polished wooden surface.

Luke didn't care. He could use his hands.

He dove upon the man, taking him to the floor and mounting him. From this position he continued to lay into him, punching one fist, then the other, then the other, then the other.

All the man could do was shield his face with his arms.

He'd seen this happen on the UFC when he watched it late at night. This would be the point the referee would decide *enough*, would shove Luke off him and wave his arms in the air.

But this was no sport.

Not for Luke, anyway.

The taste of blood incensed the man. He took the opportunity in the exchange between Luke's fists to send his own flying up into the underside of the little squirt's jaw, forcing him onto his back.

He stood, as did Luke, and they faced each other.

Two competitors.

Ready to take it to the bloody end.

And there could only be one winner.

LUKE HAD NEVER SHIED AWAY FROM A FIGHT.

In fact, at school, he had invited them.

He had been scared, at first. But then you grow to realise that one punch won't shatter you like glass.

It'll hurt, absolutely.

But it will not break you.

A punch is a punch. It is a short-term wince for a long-term target. It is the needed pain to achieve victory.

Most of those he fought had tattoos on their necks, lines in their hair, menace in their blood. They'd been fighting since they were kids, whether against their abusive step-father or the weight of their way of life.

And this entitled rich prick thought he could live up to them?

Those people fought dirty, fought hard, sent punches like they were Christmas cards.

What had this guy ever had to fight for?

The man sneered, grinning an unsettling grin, licking a spot of blood from his lip.

Luke was not afraid.

That's what he kept telling himself.

So what if this guy had killed loads of people?

So what if those trophies were of the many he'd succeeded in hurting?

Luke would wager a large amount of his drug dealing money that this guy had never fought anyone like him before.

He probably just focussed on women. On anyone he could out-muscle.

No one outmuscled Luke.

And *no one* out-angered him.

Luke was permanently pissed off at everyone.

Gray.

His dad.

Himself.

He'd been preparing for this fight for twenty-one years.

He lifted his lip into a snarl, letting out a low growl as he did.

He began his approach, stepping slowly toward the man, his fists by his side, curled and ready.

The man didn't back up, nor did he advance. He just stood, waiting for him, like a prom date about to be fucked.

Luke dove upon the man, retracting his elbow for as much leverage as he could manage and forcing his tightened knuckles into the side of the man's jaw.

The man fell to the floor.

He didn't cover his face. Didn't get up. Didn't go down further. Just crouched in the position Luke's thump had forced him into.

He didn't dab his lip, didn't feel for his swollen jaw.

He just waited for the next thump.

As if he liked being pummelled.

Luke retracted his arm once again and laid his fist into the back of the man's skull, so hard he could feel the bone shake beneath the strength of his strike.

Why wasn't this piece of shit fighting back?

Luke held his hand back again and slammed it back down once more.

This time, the man flattened onto his front.

Luke lifted his foot and flattened it into the back of the man's head.

The man was spread out, face on the floor, arms beside his head. He wasn't covering himself, protecting himself, he was just laid out, letting it happen.

The man's body began convulsing.

At first, Luke thought he was crying.

Then he heard the chuckles. The laughter, slow and heavy, precise and clear.

This fucker is enjoying this...

"What you laughing about?" Luke demanded, his voice hard and forceful.

The man didn't respond with words.

His laughter grew more hysterical, into fits of uncontrollable laughter.

He rolled onto his back and wiped his watering eyes, leaking under the strength of his uncontrollable chuckles.

Luke slammed the heel of his shoe into the man's nose.

The man just laughed more.

Harder and harder, louder and louder.

"What the *fuck* are you laughing at?" Luke demanded again.

The man tried to answer, but ended up waving his hand in response, the laughter too much for him to be able to articulate a response.

This man is truly sick...

Luke lifted his heel again and went to stamp.

The laughter ended so abruptly it took Luke a moment to realise this distraction had allowed the man to get to his feet and run.

Luke gave chase.

Then he saw what the man was running for.

The man took the knife that had fallen from his hands and turned to Luke.

Luke couldn't skid to a halt fast enough.

The next thing he felt was the warm slide of the blade beneath his ribs.

The man's face was right next to Luke's. No laughter any more. His fake hilarity, his ill-timed amusement had done enough to distract Luke and trick him and the mistake was proving fatal.

The man's lip curled, eyes flickering with gleeful rage.

The man slid the knife back out again and stuck it into Luke's gut, then retracted it once more.

Luke's hands covered his wound, but he was unable to stop the blood from seeping through his fingers, trickling down his hands and dribbling to the floor like spilt milk.

The man stabbed Luke again, but this time didn't hold the knife in – instead, he gave a series of attacks, slicing inwards and outwards as quickly as his change of mood, hitting every part of Luke's chest.

The man then stuck his leg behind Luke's and swiped his feet from under him, landing Luke on his back.

Luke's spine and skull hit the solid floor with an impact that dizzied him.

The man stood over him, feet either side of Luke's waist, looking down at his prey.

Grinning.

Still fucking grinning.

Luke tried reaching up. He didn't know why, perhaps it was a request for mercy.

"I'm going to make this one quick," the man said.

He crouched down over Luke.

"Because I'm eager to get to your sister."

Luke's eyes widened and his head filled with an ocean of panic.

Then the man slid the knife across Luke's throat.

Luke choked and spluttered, and then it was over.

He ceased to exist any longer.

JUST AS I TOLD YOU – UNPREDICTABILITY.

He was losing, so he laughed. That laughter threw the opponent. Allowed a perfect opportunity.

Because he wasn't doing what was expected.

Luke did. Because he was boring. Because he didn't deserve his banal existence.

The man stood, discarding Luke's body as something he could clean up later, smacking his hands together as if that would rid them of the blood.

He walked down the corridor and into his walk-in wardrobe. Regrettably wiping his hand on his trousers – it *had* been a nice suit – he took the key from his pocket and unlocked it.

His suits were perfectly arranged on railings across the walls of the room. To his left were his Armanis, followed by his Canalis and his Dormeuils. Across from him was his Stuart Hughes, his Brionis, William Westmancotts, his Saint Laurents and a few Valentinos. To his right, his Burberry, Dolce & Gabbanna, Prada and his Dries Van Noten.

Removing his suit and dumping it into a hamper that he

would dispose of later, he tried to make the tough decision as to which suit he didn't mind getting ruined.

He wasn't too fond of his Brionis but, honestly, he considered Prada to be an overrated pile of shit. Almost everyone who had a little bit of money to splash had one, as if it meant trying to hunt for a lesser-known but far more delectable designer brand was going to kill them.

He took his single-breasted wool and mohair Prada suit off the rails.

As for his shirt, he opted for a Dior Homme shirt with gold thread embroidery and white cotton.

He could, of course, find an old pair of overalls from when he tried painting one of his rooms himself – something that had been a complete disaster and was promptly rectified by a relatively competent painter he'd been reluctant to allow into his house.

Or, like he had done a few times, he could find one of his aprons and cover his suit with that.

But he didn't want to.

Not this time.

This girl was too damn pretty and too damn special.

He owed it to her to be dressed in his finest – even if his finest was a piece of shit suit that was worth less than half of its extortionate price tag.

He did, however, opt for no tie.

It just didn't feel like a tie occasion.

He wanted to be slightly more informal. Show her that this was a relaxed environment, that her death may be slow and excruciating but that needn't mean they couldn't be brief casual acquaintances.

He smoothed down his shirt, fixing the sleeve together with Van Cleef & Arpels cufflinks, shaped like two silver cylinders.

He straightened his suit collar.

He opened his top button.

Because, you know, why not?

He left the room, locked the door.

Found his way back to his trophy room, locked that door too.

He wouldn't be making that mistake again.

He stepped over the boy's corpse, careful not to skid on his blood.

He made his way to the top of the stairs.

He felt like that scene in Titanic, when Jack was at the top of the stairs and he turned around and said to Rose, "How would you like to go to a real party?"

He fucking loved that film.

Maybe he'd watch it later.

But not yet.

Oh, not yet.

He was too busy.

He was giddy with excitement.

He had a date with Amber.

PART V

THE FINAL DATE

39

Elsie Michaels sat alone in her living room with nothing but a lamplight for company.

She wasn't sure what was happening. She wasn't sure why. She wasn't sure where her children were.

So often she would be alone, close her eyes, and open them again to find it was dark and Amber was sitting opposite her eating tea.

So she'd closed her eyes.

Hoping that by the time she opened them...

But they weren't. It was just darkness. Open curtains framing moonlit trees and blackened roads.

She could feel life slipping away from her in every struggled breath.

She could feel her twitching fingers no longer twitching.

She could feel – no, she *knew* – that her end was almost near.

That she didn't have long left.

And she wished to be surrounded by loving children, her three reasons for battling gathered around her, holding her hand and stroking her arm.

She wished to see Amber's face, so caring, so desperate to help. Eagerly fetching Elsie's dinner, feeding her if she had to.

Elsie had never wanted to be taken care of.

She had never wanted to be charity.

In all honesty, she had prayed for death. She had prayed to be released. This was no way to live.

Every time her child fed her, she felt humiliated; but the worst part was that she didn't have the energy to say anything.

To tell Amber *just let me go...*

That it was over.

Elsie appreciated the love, but that was all she had left. Her body had shut down, her mind was absent. She wasn't even able to talk to her children, communicate with them.

She wished to see Gray's face, beaming at her, talking about his fancy degree.

She wished to see Luke's troubled frown, and to continue to claim ignorance about the things he did.

Gray and Luke – how could she have raised two boys so immensely different?

One looking to be a teacher, one who was kicked out of school.

One who was going to make his money through the result of his education, and one who was going to make his money by...

Again, she pleaded ignorance.

She tried calling out Amber's name.

Amber...

Amber...

Amber...

She heard herself calling it, but only in her head.

She felt her lips shake in an attempt to form the syllables, but those syllables never surfaced.

Strange, really.

In the past year she'd had a hundred conversations with Amber. About her ambitions, hopes, cares, work, childhood.

Only, none of those conversations had been spoken aloud.

She'd had to form her words then imagine the response.

Sometimes Amber would talk to her. She wouldn't be able to make out every word – that girl had always spoken at such a quick pace. But there was always some resemblance of sense in there, some form of coherence.

Amber, where are you...

Even when spoken in her mind, her words still sounded weak. Like a broken wheeze, or the strain of a lost voice.

Once, she was a powerful business woman. She was left in charge of a company. She would never let anyone push her around, never take any shit – she was a strong, powerful woman, like she'd always hoped to be. She'd been insistent that she would show Amber what you could accomplish in a world dominated by testosterone. She would show Amber how a woman should be – never letting anyone push you around, condescend, or deny you opportunities.

Now what?

What role model was she now?

She was the epitome of illness. The image of disease.

Her once smooth, impenetrable skin was now coarse like the surface of a screwed-up piece of paper.

She was as pale now as she would be when dead.

Her arm that once led a meeting full of intimidated men – that arm was now a dead weight, sunk upon her leg with the weight of a short life lived.

Amber...

It was no good.

Amber couldn't hear her thoughts, even if she was in the same room.

It looked like she was on her own.

Her breath faltered.
Her heartbeat slowed.
And she tried to hold on.

40

For a house so big, there were so few hiding places.

The niggling voice at the back of Amber's head told her to stop trying to find a hiding place. Told her to think about the long-game.

If she hid, she'd eventually be found.

It may be in minutes, it may be in hours, it may even be in days.

Somehow, sometime, he would find her.

She needed to find a way out. Use the time Luke had given her effectively in finding an escape.

She hoped Luke had beaten this guy, that for once his violent streak had an upside. That he had protected them both and that she needn't find a way out and that he would appear any moment declaring himself the victor and assuring Amber that she needn't worry anymore.

But for her part, Luke had given her specific instructions.

Get out.

Get help.

Only, there was no *out*...

There was no *help*...

There were only walls and expensive furniture and heavy doors and the body of her eldest brother laid out on the floor at the bottom of the stairs.

The stairs.

A creak.

She didn't move. Kept completely still.

Listened.

Footsteps, treading lightly down the stairs. Wanting to stay hidden.

But whose footsteps were they, and who were they staying hidden from?

Normally, she could recognise footsteps. If she was sat in her own living room, she would know who was coming down the stairs by the sound of the feet on the steps. Her mum would always have two hits on each step – first her foot, then the base of her slipper.

Gray's steps always sounded chaotic. There was no rhythm to his steps. There'd be a few in quick succession, then a few more, like he was always falling.

Luke's steps were heavy. Stomp, stomp, stomp. You could hear Luke's footsteps coming from the garden.

That was why she was so confused now.

She couldn't recognise the step. It was being deliberately light, intentionally soft – and there was no way she could distinguish between the creeping of the man and the creeping of Luke.

She waited, hoping that the owner of the light steps would reveal itself.

One part of her told her to run. That it could be the man, that she could be in imminent danger, and she should flee.

The other part told her it could be Luke. That she should run from her immobile stance and jump into his arms, thankful that he was still alive.

The steps left the stairs and placed themselves on the floor beside Gray's body. A tut announced itself – either at the disgust of seeing their brother, or the inconvenience of a body that hadn't cleared itself up yet.

The steps approached.

She pressed herself up against the wall, flattening out, keeping herself unseen, inches from the door frame.

The steps approached the doorway where they paused.

Waiting.

Looking for something, maybe. Listening. Trying to hear whether Amber was near.

She wanted to turn around and throw herself into Luke's arms, to hold him tight and tell him she loved him and beg for him to help her get out of this hell house.

But what if it wasn't Luke?

A hand reached around the door frame toward Amber's head.

Amber wondered what it was doing, then she realised she was covering the light switch. With as much stealth as she could manage, she ducked silently out of the way and allowed the hand to flick the light switch, to illuminate the room in artificial light, revealing a grand dining table on one side and a pristine kitchen on the other.

She stared at the hand for the brief moment it passed her eyes.

It had a suit blazer. A white shirt. Cufflinks.

It was not the tracksuit of Luke's attire.

It was not Luke.

She closed her eyes, pressed them together, holding her breath to avoid making even the slightest sound.

The owner of the hand stepped in, pausing after a few steps. Hands on hips, he looked around.

Amber covered her own mouth to stifle her breathing.

She watched the back of his head, praying that he did not turn around.

HE KNEW SHE WAS THERE.

He was not an idiot.

This was all part of the thrills.

The chase, the taunting, the playing. The moments where you give them hope, just before the moment where you take it away.

He stepped into the kitchen, listening to the stifled breaths behind him. If he wasn't so attuned to such muffled whimpers he wouldn't have heard them – as it was, the small cries of a hiding woman were a ringing bell to him, except a lot more pleasant to listen to.

He opened a kitchen cupboard, took out a glass and placed it beneath the tap.

Mixing with the sounds of the water rising in pitch as the glass filled, were the small patters of gently creeping feet upon the tiled surface of a kitchen floor.

She was trying to edge out of the room.

He grinned.

He wondered how he should do this.

Should he let her hope for a little longer?

He gulped down the pint of water in mere seconds. This was thirsty work, and his head was aching from the mild pounding he'd had to receive. He rubbed the back of his neck, worrying that he had pulled a muscle.

He finished his large gulp of water with a satisfying "ah", dropped the pint glass in the sink, and placed his hands on the side, looking at the girl's reflection in the metal surface of the tap.

Despite the shape of the tap distorting her, she was still looking quite pretty. She looked young, probably younger than she was – he wouldn't have been surprised to find out she was still at school.

He'd never killed a girl that young before.

He wasn't that kind of murderer.

He despised paedophiles. They disgusted him. They were the gutter of the world of torture.

That didn't mean anything would change with the girl, though.

She may look young, but he was certain she wasn't.

Young girls don't have this kind of fight in them.

Young girls just close their eyes and don't know what's happening.

Her reflection contorted and displaced as she pushed herself around the doorway, gripping the wall, treading so lightly she thought she hadn't been noticed.

He turned and strode, not in the way of the girl, but in the other way, across the long length of the kitchen to another door, a door that he unlocked and entered.

He entered the library, paced through the music room and the television room, walking a full circle around the ground floor in the opposite way to Amber.

He paused by the door way, watching, Gray still deceased at the base of the stairs.

He saw her creep from the kitchen, along the wall, toward the stairs, thinking she was safe.

Thinking he was still in the kitchen.

Thinking she wasn't being watched.

Thinking there was no one about to step out, reveal themselves, and begin the end of her life.

42

AMBER DIDN'T MOVE.

She could feel her breathing getting heavier, but she silenced it as best she could.

He didn't falter or flinch, so he mustn't have heard it. He couldn't have.

He took out a glass and filled it up.

He had blood all over his skin.

On his hands. On his face. On his neck.

Was that Luke's blood?

My God, where is Luke...

Did this mean this guy won? That Luke was dead?

He didn't have to be dead.

Luke could be incapacitated. Prisoner. Handcuffed, bound, shoved somewhere Amber could later discover.

Or was this just denial all over again?

The man slammed his glass down and gave a relieved "ah." He dropped the glass in the sink and leant his hands on the side.

He seemed to stare at the tap. Dementedly staring, fixed by it, as if the tap was about to move or dance or do something.

Amber had an image of him ripping the tap off, turning to her and using it to beat her to death.

She couldn't wait any longer.

She placed one foot on the floor, careful to soften her gentle step on the tiles, then shuffled along, slowly and steadily creeping out of the room.

Her eyes never moved from the back of the guy's head.

She was worried he'd turn around. People can always seem to tell when someone is staring at them. At any moment he could turn around, lock eyes with her, and any chance of survival would be over.

Having made it out of the room, she crept along the wall until he was out of sight.

She paused, breathing out the breath she was holding.

The relief was halted by the reminder that all she'd done was move a room away from him.

She was still only yards away.

Yards away from a sadistic, twisted killer.

And, as if she needed a reminder, Gray's body still lay absently on the floor.

Should she go search for Luke's body? To make sure?

Then what?

If he was alive, what would she do?

If he was dead, what would she do?

She moved toward the stairs, stepping over Gray as if she was getting used to the sight but she wasn't, she couldn't, she refused to let herself be used to it.

She mentally insisted that the sight of her dead brother would always horrify her, would always give her nightmares – she refused to believe anything else.

She would not get used to his corpse.

But Gray's pale face and wide open mouth had remained in place for almost an hour now, stiffening.

"I know," came a gentleman's voice.

At first, Amber felt relief. She believed it was someone come to help her. The voice was just so well-spoken and so kind that there was no way the owner of such a voice could harm her.

This was it.

Someone had found a way in. They had heard the screams, or they were just passing by, a post-man maybe, or even better, a police officer.

She even felt herself smiling, felt her breathing calming, such was the delusion her defence mechanism.

Even as she looked into his face, it didn't register.

The blood splatter across his bruised cheek, the crusted blood on his neck, and the bloody grin beaming back at her.

Then it registered.

And she screamed.

Boy, did she scream.

Loud. High-pitched. Piercing.

Even the man flinched – but in a mocking way. The way you would when your baby has just dribbled their food down their bib, and you say *silly you* as you wipe it up for them.

She turned and ran.

He kicked his leg up, smacking it into hers, sending her legs sprawling in the air before landing on Gray's cracked spine.

She scrambled her feet off the body, not just out of fear, but out of an instinct not to touch the corpse, not to affect it in any way.

She pushed herself to a crawl, then pushed herself to a stumbling run, and scrambled her way back through the room and through to the kitchen.

She looked over her shoulder.

He wasn't following.

Why wasn't he following?

If anything, this unnerved her more than if he was chasing her.

Now, she couldn't see him.

It was as if he knew something that she didn't.

43

As soon as she ran, he turned and strode mercilessly back through the television room, the music room and the library, returning to the door he'd used to sneak out of the kitchen seconds ago.

He did not enter it – no, he simply locked it to avoid chasing her in circles, then walked back on himself once more.

Past the library full of books he'd never read.

Back through the music room with a piano that was just for show.

Back through the television that only showed news he didn't care for.

Past the body he'd clean up later.

When were those fucking pigs arriving?

Sort it later.

Back through the kitchen to find her standing in front of the door he'd locked, pulling on its handle then punching her body into it.

She looked at him and didn't move.

Wide-eyed.

Pale faced.

Mortified.

The sight gave him an erection that convulsed under his increasing pulse.

Both of them, like a stand-off in a western, stood, staring, waiting to see what the other did.

Well, Amber was waiting to see what he did.

He was just enjoying her confusion. Savouring her terror. Relishing her fatal indecision.

"What do you want?" she questioned, so faintly he barely heard it.

"You'll have to speak up, my dear," he answered, trying not to grin so hard.

"I said, what do you want?" she repeated, this time with more assertion, though it was fake assertion.

He took a step forward.

She tried to take a step back but just ended up flattening against the door.

My God, she is so scared.

He could have done anything and she'd panic. He could sneeze, laugh, sneer – any movement would make her cry or scream or beg for mercy.

Never had someone been so under his control, so easily manipulated, so completely stumped by fear.

It felt good.

It felt so fucking good.

"Amber, is it?" he asked.

She turned her head, figuring him out, wondering what his game was.

"Well?" he said, prompting an answer.

"Yes…" she whispered.

"Your brothers, they… They really loved you."

"What?"

"I said, your brothers, they loved you. Wouldn't shut up about you the whole time."

She still didn't move.

Still.

How could someone remain so motionless?

"Did you kill Luke?"

He chuckled.

"Are you going to come away from that door any time soon?" he asked.

"Did you kill Luke?"

"Amber, my darling – what do you think?"

Her head dropped, her eyes closed, her body shook. Everything crushed her. She looked like she was huddling to shelter from heavy rain, yet the droplets were still falling upon her like bullets and there was nothing she could do. Her face curled up into a really ugly grimace, like every feature was morphing toward her nose.

He was starting to get bored.

In a moment of sudden inspiration, she leapt to a nearby kitchen draw, opened it and immediately found a sharp bread knife.

Ah, wonderful. Just as she was starting to get boring, she made it a bit more exciting.

"Don't come anywhere fucking near me!" she shouted.

It was like a museum of emotions. One moment she was quiet and timid, then inconsolable, then angry. He wondered what would come next – horny?

Sighing, he pulled out a seat at the table and sat down. He rested his head on his hand, one finger pointing up his cheek, his right foot upon his left knee.

And he watched her.

Sat, waiting for the entertainment to begin.

"I mean it!" she insisted, pointing the knife at him. "I fucking mean it!"

"Amber, do I look like I'm coming anywhere near you?" he said, raising a hand to remonstrate how stupid she was being.

She just held the knife forward, edging closer to him, albeit with the intention of being closer to the door.

"How do I get out?"

He said nothing. Just watched her.

"How do I get out?"

Yawned.

"I said how do I get out?"

Still watching. Keep on watching. Watch watch watching.

"Just answer me, how?" The toughened resolve she had somehow found the first three times she had asked had gone, and the final request was more of a crying plea. "Please, lift these shutters. Let me go."

"Is this honestly your approach? You're going to plead with me to death?"

"I'll stab you!"

"And then what? How will you get out then? You'll starve in here. Maybe not straight away, there is food – but not enough. All you'll have is you and the other bodies to keep you company."

She flinched.

"What, you think you're the only ones?"

She flinched again.

"No, you don't, do you?" He clapped his hands joyously together. "You wily dog, you've seen them! Haven't you? Sheila and Eve, upstairs."

"Sheila is the girl on the news…"

"Yes. Yes, she is. And Eve is just a whore, if that helps. Albeit, a very good whore, in the way that only really expensive whores are – but a whore, nonetheless."

"You're sick. Crazy."

He shrugged.

"Is that supposed to offend me, Amber? You think there's anything you can do here that would surprise me or work against me? You think I haven't heard the pleas or the threats, or that I haven't witnessed the sight of some little girl holding a knife that shakes so hard she'll probably do more damage to herself than me?"

He stood.

She held the quivering knife tighter.

"Don't you come any closer!"

"Amber, please," he said, coming closer. "We're past this now, don't you think?"

"I will stab you! I mean it!"

"I'm sure you do." He stepped forward, reaching his hand out. "But I'm getting bored of this now."

She backed away until she was up against the door once more. She tried it, finding it locked, then tried it again, then tried it once more.

And she says I'm the crazy one?

He reached a hand out, his palm open.

"Give me the knife, Amber."

She held it out to him.

He approached.

"Give it to me."

She refused.

His hand approached her wrist.

"Give me the knife."

She lunged and he caught her and he smacked her wrist against the fridge so hard the knife went clattering into somewhere unknown.

His hand clasped around her neck and he knew he could just end it all here but that was not what he wanted.

That was definitely not what he wanted.

Her brothers had been quick – but that was only so he could get to her. The crappy starters before the glorious main.

"Please..." she continued to beg.

Why?

Why beg?

Don't disgrace yourself.

Don't bemoan yourself a good death.

A good death is a reward. It is a unique thing that only comes to those deserved.

And she was deserving.

She went to plead again, but he rendered her unable by hitting her head three times, hard, against the door, and dropping her unconscious body to the ground.

44

"Amber, wake up," came the eager voice of Elsie Michaels.

"What?" Amber replied, rubbing the fuzz out of her sleepy eyes.

"Amber, it's your birthday."

Was it?

Since when?

What?

"Come on, Amber, wake up."

Feeling her mum pulling on her arm, Amber sat up and turned, placing her feet down and watching the tufts of carpet find their way between the gaps of her tiny toes.

Her pyjamas had pictures of dinosaurs on them.

All the boys at school always took the mickey out of her boyish interests, as did her brothers, but she liked dinosaurs and not barbies and so why shouldn't she wear dinosaur pyjamas?

Only, she hadn't worn these pyjamas for almost ten years.

"Come on," Elsie said, grabbing Amber's hand and taking her down the stairs.

She was half the size of her mum.

Her mum, dressed in her suit for work, her blond, spritely hair tied back, her makeup subtly applied. The power-woman, the business woman – the role model every young girl should have.

She entered the kitchen where a cake waited for her.

She counted the candles.

One. Two. Three. Four. Five. Six. Seven. Eight. Nine.

Nine.

This was her ninth birthday.

But she didn't feel nine.

"Are you going to blow them out?"

She looked uncomfortably from herself to her mum, who looked back so enthusiastically, so desperate for this day to be special.

But Amber didn't understand.

She wasn't nine.

This wasn't her birthday.

Seeing the expectant look on her mum's face and not wanting to upset her, she blew out the candles and went to sit – but Elsie pulled on her arm again.

"No time to eat it yet, you have presents to open!"

She led Amber through the hallway and into the living room.

It was incredible.

Balloons covered the entire room, bouncing between Luke and Gray. Luke still played with them, but Gray was sat in the corner with his arms folded like the grumpy teenager he was becoming.

S Club Juniors were playing in the background. Amber had loved them at nine, but outgrew them at ten.

A mass of presents took up so much of the room. So many presents.

Her mum was usually sat asleep in the corner of this room, but there she was, in her thirties, vibrant, sparkling. Showing

Amber into the room full of presents, full of gifts that Elsie was so insistent Amber deserved.

"What do you think?"

Amber didn't know what to say.

"I just wanted your day to be perfect."

Her day?

She wasn't nine.

It wasn't her day.

Her mum was sick. Ill. Dying desperately in the confines of a cold, empty house they could no longer afford.

"Mum," Amber said, her voice a child's voice. "What is happening?"

"What do you mean, darling?"

"I just…this… This isn't right…"

"Oh, you are becoming a big girl. Come here!"

Elsie pulled Amber close and fastened her arms around her.

Her mum's hugs had always been the best hugs. So warm and tight. They practically suffocated you but that's what Amber loved about them. So many people hugged because they had to, just perching their hands on someone's arms and briefly embracing them. Mum was the complete opposite. If she hugged you, she wanted you to know you'd been hugged.

As much as Amber wished to object, she couldn't.

She hadn't realised how much she'd missed these hugs.

She put her arms around Mum too, holding on, her fingers sticking into her back as she gripped her and refused to let her go.

But she was crying.

Amber was crying.

"Amber."

She hadn't realised it, but she was.

Why was she crying?

But she knew why.

"Amber, wake up."

It's because she was right.

She wasn't nine.

This wasn't her birthday.

And Elsie Michaels was still sat in her chair, dying in a home without heating.

"Amber, come on, you're being rude now."

And, as Amber's eyes opened, she saw the reality of where she was.

Then it got worse.

45

SHE EVEN WEPT WHEN SHE SLEPT.

It was like he couldn't get a break from it.

He'd knocked her unconscious for a moment's peace from the whining and the begging and the pleading and the whinging, just so he could do what he needed to do, but *no*.

I mean, he was planning a surprise for her.

A *surprise!*

An elaborate ruse he'd been desperate to get ready for her awakening.

But the whole way through it this – this ungrateful... ungrateful little... ungrateful little *bitch* just wouldn't shut up with this and that and this and that and oh dear God!

"Elsie..." she moaned, pushing her head to one side, then back to the other.

It was about the only thing she could push. It wasn't like any other part of her was moveable.

"Elsie... No... Elsie..."

Elsie?

"I'm not nine... not nine..."

He laughed.

The weird things people dream…

"It's not my birthday…"

He laughed again.

He had a girlfriend once who was insistent that he spoke in his sleep. Not just spoke – but had full on conversations with no one and shouted out random things. Apparently, once he had even woken her up by biting her. She had screamed but he hadn't noticed and wasn't aware of it until the following morning when she filled him in.

"Elsie… The cake…"

He studied her for a moment. Her peaceful eyes as unpeaceful as one can get. She should be asleep, unconscious, at one with silence – instead she was rattling on her nonsensical ramblings.

He'd arranged the scene as he wanted it.

As he would hope she would want it.

This was going to be perfect.

He had planned it perfectly.

Ever since he'd seen her in the reflection of the tap, skew-whiff yet perfect, he'd known.

He'd always wanted to do this – he'd just never had the opportunity. His women had always been alone, never with others.

He couldn't wait to see the look on her face.

"Elsie…"

She was crying.

Actually, properly crying.

In her sleep, her eyes shut tight, but with snail trails running down her cheeks.

She looked fucking ugly when she cried.

Don't we all?

The scene was arranged.

The surprise was ready.

He took his seat. He clasped his hands beneath his chin and

watched Amber, waiting for her to come around and see the perfect world he'd created.

"Amber," he said.

She continued to toss back and forth, one side to the other, her head twisting and by George if she doesn't pull a muscle she'd be lucky.

"Amber, wake up."

She winced and struggled more.

Her eyes began to flicker.

There she was.

He waited.

And waited.

"Amber, come on, you're being rude now."

Her eyes opened.

She looked at him first and he saw the recognition in her face. A frantically tired recognition, a resolve met with horror.

He wondered if she'd rather the nightmare.

Then she looked at her surprise.

He couldn't help but beam as she screamed.

And boy, did she scream.

She screamed like no other ever had.

He'd heard screams before, don't get me wrong – he'd heard a lot of them.

All kinds of screams.

Loud ones, quiet ones.

High-pitched, low-pitched.

Gutteral, manly, womanly, odd, bizarre intonations, flexing tones, distant, close, elongated and short.

But he'd never heard a scream like this.

And, in her bewildered eyes, he decided it was all worth it. The effort he'd put into her elaborate awakening all fell into place, and that look of meaningless terror she had, that look like things couldn't be worse and then she suddenly realised they damn well could be – that look would stay with him forever.

It was the favourite look he'd ever seen.

"Who's–" he went to ask, but the screaming started up again.

He waved his arms and leant back.

"Fine, I'll just wait until you're done."

She looked around herself, as if purposefully trying to give herself a reason to scream, then her voice went, turned into a cry, and she finally shut up.

"Lovely," he said, and waited another moment to see if she was going to start again.

She didn't.

She just dropped her head and wept.

He could finally ask his question.

"Who's Elsie, Amber?"

46

SHE KNEW THE HOUSE SHE WAS IN.

She knew the smug face that sat across the table from her.

But she hadn't expected this.

He looked so happy about it. So pleased, like his terrific plan had formed into a monumental image he knew would horrify the final moments of her existence.

She screamed.

What else could she do?

She kept looking between them.

From Luke's face.

To Gray's face.

And back again.

Propped up at the table.

Luke to her left, Gray to her right.

On the table was a spread of food with a floral teapot and empty cups beside plates laid out before her, him, Luke and Gray.

Luke and Gray both wore bibs.

Gray's face was already white. He sat upright without support, his body already with enough stiffness to hold him still. His eyes were held open with duct tape but his pupils did not correspond with each other, both of them falling to the opposite corner of his eyes.

Similarly, Luke sat upright, but was held in place with rope. His head flopped but she could still see the hooks pulling his mouth into a wide grin. A playful grin. Like he was enjoying the tea party.

Like they all were.

And him. The man. The owner of this fortress of a mansion.

He sat opposite, his head resting on his clasped hands, his face still grinning that same fucking grin that hadn't left his face since she first saw him.

She tried to look away from them.

From her brothers.

"Who's–" the man went to speak.

She screamed.

She didn't want to hear it.

She made herself look at the cold faces of her brothers coerced into this sick position to intentionally fill her up with fear, to help create a scream that would outdo the volume of his voice.

He waved his hands like she was being unreasonable.

"Fine, I'll just wait until you're done."

Eventually, her voice went.

She felt it dissipate back into her throat, felt her neck tighten, and found that all she could do was cry.

She let her head drop.

Her dead brothers stared at her.

Watched her with judgemental eyes that just seconds ago seemed like they were having such a nice time at this...

Whatever this was.

This sick, twisted tea party.

What the fuck is this...

Her mum, sat at home, dying and alone, popped into her head in a subtle image that caused her to weep some more.

"Who's Elsie, Amber?" he asked.

She lifted her head. How did he know that name?

"Who is Elsie?" he repeated.

"How do you…"

"You were saying it in your sleep. Over and over. Rather repetitive, but it intrigued me. Who is Elsie?"

She considered whether to tell him, then thought that maybe she could suffer one last attempt to reach any heart that may beat inside this man's chest.

"She's our mother," she said, spitting it out, each word an angry struggle.

"Your mother?"

"She's dying."

"Oh dear, I am sorry to hear that."

She wanted to snap at him, to demand how he could ever understand what it's like to be hurt by someone else's death when he surrounded himself with it and celebrated it so dearly.

"That's why we are here," she said instead, hoping he would understand. "Our only chance is a drug trial… It costs thirteen thousand pounds…"

"Ah!" He clicked his fingers and swung his arm like a sudden moment of clarity had become him. "Well, why didn't you say so?"

Why didn't I say so?

What did he mean?

"I offer money to many causes like yours," he said. "If you'd have just asked, or applied for a grant via my business's website, I'd have happily helped."

"What…"

Was she hearing this right?

He would help?

She could have applied for a grant?

"I said I would be happy to help, Amber."

"You would?"

"Of course. I promise that I will see to it your mother receives the treatment she requires. What was her name again?"

"Elsie... Michaels..."

"Elsie Michaels! What a lovely name to besmirch such an unfortunate woman. Well, Amber, here is what I'll do – I'll give it a day or two for this to die over, then I will go visit her and give her the money she needs."

"You will..."

Was he toying with her?

Somehow, this was the cruellest torment yet.

"Of course, of course! I mean, you've all been such lovely guests." He raised his hands to indicate the two corpses propped up beside him.

She shook her head. Cried. Wept.

"Stop it..." she said, closing her eyes and dropping her head to one side. It was only now that she realised she was bound by rope. Funny how she hadn't thought to move until now.

"I'm being serious, Amber. *Deadly* serious. Do you not know who I am?"

"No..."

"My name is Gerald Brittle, my dear. Surely you've heard of me?"

Gerald Brittle.

The name sounded so familiar.

Gerald Brittle. Gerald Brittle.

Then the recollections hit her.

He owned the Brittle empire, a business that ran so many other businesses, from security firms to shops to therapists to warehouses to manufacturers to... well, just about anything.

And they did have a grant.

The Brittle Grant.

It was famous for helping people like her.

He was someone who could help.

"Do you understand now? Your mother is going to be fine."

Amber seemed to forget where she was and what was happening for a moment, and she smiled, a grateful, happy smile.

"Unfortunately," Gerald said. "You will not be around to see it."

GERALD WATCHED THE SMILE FADE AND THE LIGHTS GO OUT IN Amber's eyes.

He watched any contentment or hope fade from her body.

He would be true to his word.

He *would* save her mother.

And she *would not* be around to see it.

He stood, made his way across the table, and loitered behind her. She tried turning her head to see him but she couldn't turn it enough.

A box, connected to the wall, hung beside the door. He hit a code, it opened, and he flicked a switch.

Slowly, every shutter that surrounded the house lifted. The early morning sun illuminated the room in a happy haze, casting a loving glow on his homely kitchen.

He placed his hands on his hips and gazed out upon his garden.

His watch beeped.

His morning alarm.

He was going to be late for work.

"Oh, shucks," he said, his body dropping. "I was hoping to take this slow..."

She was looking around herself so quickly, so hopeful, so pleased to see the sun.

It was so sweet.

Bless her.

Bless her in her little cotton socks, as his grandmother used to say.

He was going to have to get this over with.

"Are you – are you letting me go?" she asked.

Did she not just hear what he said?

"I literally just said you are going to die, Amber."

He shook his head.

Impudent girl.

Rubbing his eyes, he made his way to the coffee maker. He was going to need caffeine. He'd been up all night, and he hadn't been particularly restful. He could hardly skip out on work – he had a big deal potentially going ahead. Not only did he have to go in, he was going to need all the energy he could get.

He looked at the two brothers propped up at the table.

How had he lost track of time so much?

He was still going to have to clean this all up...

He took the phone off the wall and dialled a number.

"*We are sorry, but the outgoing call function has been disabled at this time.*"

He pressed a button.

"*Outgoing call function enabled.*"

"Hi, Brad, I'm going to be half an hour or so late, please tell the clients to wait... Thanks a bunch, you're a star."

He hung up.

For some reason, Amber was watching him with her mouth agape. It looked rather odd. Like she was trying to open her mouth as wide as she could or something.

Catching flies – another of his grandmother's sayings.

The coffee maker finished. He took his cup, sipped on it, and relished it.

Bad coffee tastes like horseshit.

But good coffee tastes like heaven.

He sipped another sip.

Now that was heaven.

"Just... Just get on with it..."

He placed the cup on the side.

If he was going to manage to clean up all three of them in the time he had, he had little choice. He was going to have to get to it.

"Okay, Amber," he said. "How shall we do this?"

HE LOOKS AT HER LIKE THE LAST SLICE OF PIE.

Like a cream cake on sale.

Like butter slathered and melted over a warm slice of bread.

She feels nervous and giddy, like she's on a first date. The fear is now buried, a strange excitement overcomes her, as she knows what is about to happen.

Is this what it's like to die?

Being honest, her life wasn't much to live, was it?

Straying from one anxiety to the next, dedicating every day to earning money and taking care of her mum, despite never earning much money and her mum still deteriorating by the minute.

She tries to stop being scared.

She starts to accept her inevitable fate.

She welcomes death like an old friend, a sweet release she would enter confident that Mum would be okay.

She'd have no children, and she'd be devastated – but she'd be okay.

She knew of Gerald Brittle's willingness to help. The charitable reputation of a wonderful businessman precedes the name, and she could die happy knowing that everything would be okay.

She smiles at him, which she finds strange, but he smiles back and suddenly everything feels okay.

His terrifying eyes are warm.

His hostile hands are soft.

Her death will be sweet and he will relish it and she will hope that it's over quickly.

He doesn't waste any more time. He charges at her with something he takes from a kitchen draw that she can't quite make out, but it's big and it's metal and maybe it's her salvation.

Gerald strikes her over the head with it and the impact turns the room to an underwater haze. Her chair topples over and she smacks her cheek on the cold kitchen floor.

She doesn't struggle against the ropes.

Why bother?

She wouldn't get out.

The morning sun shines in her eyes but it's an amber blur. An orange glow she can just about deduce.

Gerald screams as he strikes again.

This time it's on her cranium and this time it really hurts and this time the room disappears to a melancholy soundtrack of the most emotional part of a film.

Like Finding Nemo. Her mum's favourite film.

What a strange film to be a middle-aged business woman's favourite.

Amber closes her eyes, waiting for the next impact, and it arrives on time just like she knew it would.

Then the next comes and she disappears.

She listens to the strikes hit her, but she doesn't feel them anymore.

She's empty.

A vessel.

The broken words of a soon-to-be-forgotten mind.

How long will this last?

She hears the strikes becoming more frequent, harder, burying her head that she somehow knows has caved in.

The side of her head is indented into her brain.

Her fingers twitch.

She feels nothing else, but she feels that.

She misses her mum.

She misses her brothers.

But she's had enough.

She tries to cry but she's no longer able.

She tries to laugh but the chuckles are stifled.

She tries to thank Gerald, to tell him not to stop, to tell him that he did the right thing in the end.

But even his grunts grow distant.

In the end she's just lying there, knowing she's dying but not caring or doing anything about it.

And then she has her final thought.

It's a memory, as most final thoughts are.

She's nine again.

It's not her birthday, it's a few weeks later.

They are in the park. Gray is too old for it so he's in the adjacent skate park, trying to do tricks with his BMX that don't quite come off and all the other teenagers laugh at him.

Luke is standing coolly at the side, just watching her.

Elsie Michaels stands behind her, pushing her on the swing, pushing her hard so she can fly high.

She always pushed hard, and Amber always flew high.

Amber is giggling. Her mum is laughing too.

It's the kind of image you'd hang on your wall.

Her mum slows down.

Amber doesn't look around, she just shouts, "More! More!"

But there is no more.

Luke is behind her.

Somehow, Gray is behind her.

They've both rushed over.

Amber puts her feet on the ground and stops the swing and she turns and there is her mum her mum her mum just lying on the floor just lying and she's hurt and she's seizing and there's foam coming out of her mouth and what's happening what's happening what's going on with her please mum be okay please mum please mum please...

But she isn't okay.

She won't be okay for a long time.

Not until some wealthy businessman steps in and saves her.

And the memory ended.

She was back in the room.

Except, she wasn't.

Her mind shut down.

And she ended.

PART VI

THE MOST GENEROUS MAN IN THE WORLD

DETECTIVE CONSTABLE JOHN DANIELS FINISHED OFF HIS conversation with Elsie Michaels, feeling annoyed that he hadn't really made any progress, and feeling annoyed for feeling that way.

She was desperately ill, there were no qualms about it. Unfortunately, this meant that getting much conversation out of her was proving difficult, and he was forced to end his questions as she fell asleep.

He wondered how long she had left.

He promised her they would do all they could do find her daughter and two sons, but he wasn't sure she understood or heard him.

Then again, he had an aunt who was sick once. He'd spoken to her despite her looking like she wasn't listening. He'd given a full monologue beside her death bed about the troubles he was having at school.

Then, on the day she died, her eyes woke and declared that he should stand up to the bullies then she faded away again.

You never know what they hear.

A Mercedes pulled up outside the house and Daniels couldn't help but smile.

Any time there was a sick person in such desperate need and that car pulled up, he felt like jumping for joy.

The door opened and out he stepped. Rich philanthropist and modern-day saint, Gerald Brittle.

"Morning, Detective," he said, nodding his head toward Daniels.

Daniels couldn't help but gush. It was bizarre, really – this was just a man. But it was just what this man had done for society, it was...

Overwhelming.

That was the only word for it.

"Good morning, Mr Brittle."

"Please," Gerald said, smoothing down the sleeves of his pristine suit and flashing his bright, white teeth in a charming, suave smile. "Call me Gerald."

Daniels was so pleased he got to call him Gerald.

"Where is Miss Michaels?" Gerald asked. "Is she in here?"

Daniels shook his head in astonishment.

"God bless you, Mr Brittle. I mean, Gerald." He held his hand out to direct Gerald toward the house. "Right in there."

"Thank you," Gerald said, flashing that millionaire smile again.

"Let me get the door for you," Daniels insisted, and rushed to the door, opening it.

Gerald nodded at him and he gushed again.

Then Daniels stood in the doorway, just at the right angle to see through the crack of the living room door, so he could see the marvellous exchange that was about to happen.

Gerald stepped into the living room and paused. Looked at Elsie Michaels and held his hands out wide.

"Well, Miss Michaels," he exclaimed, loud enough and

joyous enough to prompt her to lift her head from her impenetrable snooze. "It is lovely to see you."

Elsie managed a slight frown, a moment of confusion, but Gerald let it pass. He walked up to her and crouched before her, taking her cold hands in his.

"And how are you?" Gerald asked.

Elsie just stared back at him.

"Don't worry, that was a stupid question," Gerald admitted. "And you're right not to have the energy to answer it. Listen, Elsie – can I call you Elsie?"

She faintly nodded her head.

This woman who couldn't react to any of Daniels' officers was somehow responding to this man.

How did he do it?

"My name is Gerald Brittle, have you heard of me?"

She didn't move, but her eyes said yes.

"Perfect. I heard about your case and I just had to help. I had to. How could I not?"

He smiled at her so smoothly Daniels almost gushed on Elsie's behalf.

"And there is a drug trial I want to enter you in. And I am not only going to pay for the trial, I am going to pay for whatever home or aftercare you need afterwards. I am going to pay whatever is needed to help you feel better, is that all right?"

A small tear trickling down her cheek was his answer.

"Oh, come on," Gerald said, wrapping his arms around her – not so tight as to hurt her, but close enough that she would know he was there.

Daniels wished he could do what Gerald did.

He rued his wage, and his limited means of helping.

If only all the rich were like Gerald, this world would be a much better place.

"I will help you Elsie," Gerald said. "No matter what."

Daniels had to wipe his own tear away.
What a wonderful man.
God bless this man.
God bless Gerald Brittle.

THE TO PREQUEL TO SHUTTER
HOUSE IS OUT NOW

For more on **This Book is Full of Bodies** visit
http://www.rickwoodwriter.com/shutter-house.html

ALSO IN THE BLOOD SPLATTER
BOOKS SERIES...

Psycho B*tches
Home Invasion

BLOOD SPLATTER BOOKS

18+

PSYCHO
B*TCHES

RICK WOOD

BLOOD SPLATTER BOOKS

18+

HOME
INVASION

RICK WOOD

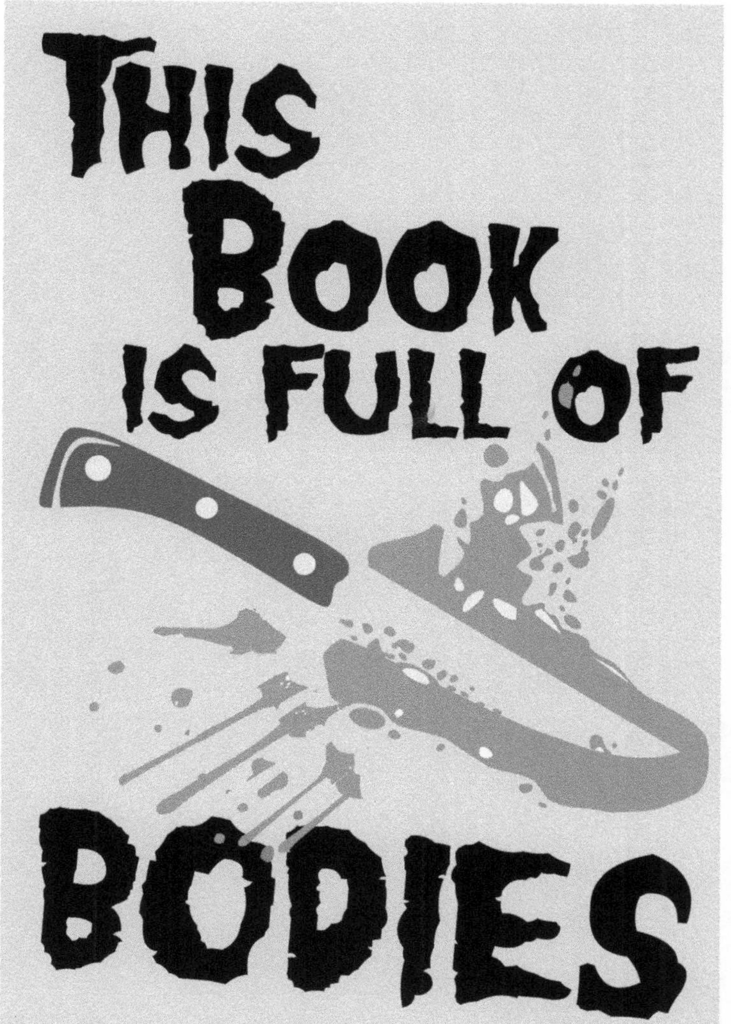
THIS BOOK IS FULL OF BODIES
RICK WOOD

JOIN RICK'S READER'S GROUP AND GET AT LEAST TWO BOOKS FOR FREE

Join at www.rickwoodwriter.com/sign-up